Artifact

D.R. Swan

This book is a work of fiction. Any resemblance to persons, places or incidents are either the product of the author's imagination or are used fictitiously, and any resemblance to actual persons, living or dead, locales or events are completely coincidental.

It's fiction. Have fun!

Artifact
By D. R. Swan

Book Cover Image By
Evan

(ar029)

Dedication

To Evan and Ryan, always foremost in my thoughts and prayers.

Acknowledgments

Thanks to everyone for their help, support, and kindness. It's been a long road, and I hope to continue to improve my writing with the help of people who care.

Artifact

Preface

January 5, 2085

In October of 2015, Earth was nearly hit by an asteroid dubbed, "The Halloween Asteroid (TB145)." No one had detected it until ten days before its approach. The skull-shaped asteroid raced by our planet with its haunting, empty eye sockets mocking us as it passed, nearly as close as the Moon and though 300,000 miles away, in astronomical terms, it was far too close for comfort. Traveling at 78,000 miles per hour and the size of a football field and a half, had it struck, it would have devastated a huge area.

Though seventy years later, little has changed to prevent a collision with these lethal objects. The world has attempted to keep tabs on asteroids that travel close to

Earth, monitored in part by Nasa's Jet Propulsion Lab, (JPL). To date, more than 20,000 have been identified.

Dubbed NEO's (Near Earth Objects), these objects are observed and categorized using ground-based telescopes, and the space-based, 50-year-old Neowise telescope and the Neowise 2, launched just two years ago (January 11, 2083). But even with that, asteroids still sneak through.

Six months ago, July 30, 2084, another asteroid came closer than the one in 2015. It was detected just four days before its pass, between the Moon and Earth.

It seems to be only a matter of time before our planet would be struck by a devastating asteroid or comet. Even a relatively small one could wreak havoc over a wide area. In 1908, a small asteroid of unknown size exploded in a remote, uninhabited area of Russia. Though no known humans were killed, over 80 million trees were flattened in an area of nearly 2000 kilometers, which is close to 1243 miles. It takes a great deal of explosive power to knock down a tree, imagine if that same asteroid had struck a city like Los Angeles or New York.

This is a real danger for the world, but the countries on this planet are too busy in conflict and bickering to address the fact that just one of these asteroids could end all life here in the only place that humans, one of the most fragile of creatures, can call home. That is until the arrival of, *"The Artifact."*

Part 1

Artifact

Chapter 1

March 30, 2085

10:15 AM PST

Nathen Maken sat at his workstation at JPL surrounded by screens that monitored Earth satellites. He had just come back from a break and still faced five hours before his shift would end. Distracted, his mind wandered from work to a first date with a woman he had met a week before in the cafeteria. She was tall and smart and had worked for JPL for the last five years and he couldn't quite understand what she saw in him, but she had said yes to a date. It would be interesting to see if he could get a second.

Nathen's mind was forced back to his work as a red light flashed on his control panel.

"What the hell?" he said quietly to himself.

He checked his instruments then typed a series of commands into his keyboard. His next words were, "Sir, we've just lost a satellite over Russia. It appears to be gone, catastrophic failure."

His supervisor, James Brady, sat at his desk and glanced up through thick, wire-rimmed glasses. He asked, "Any idea what happened?"

"No. One minute it was functioning fine, the next, it had vanished."

"Can we get a look from the Neowise 2?"

"Just a minute... Checking.... Checking... Nothing reported."

"Sir," Mark Hillman, who worked at the station next to Maken's interrupted. "Russia is reporting a meteor strike west of the Kamchatka region, heavy damage and significant loss of life. It must have taken out our satellite."

"Where did it hit? Find out where it came from and why we didn't see it."

"Yes, sir," Hillman said.

March 30, 2085

10:46 AM PST

CNN Reporter Blake Trenton: "We are just receiving word that a city in eastern Russia has been hit by a small asteroid. It struck around 10:15 AM Pacific Standard Time and has done so much damage that little information is coming out of a nearby city. Everything is down including power and all communications. The Russian government is rushing help from a nearby army base, which had also reported heavy damage. We've reached out to NASA's Jet Propulsion Laboratory for additional information, but they say that they did not detect the incoming asteroid. When asked, 'Isn't that your job?' They responded, "We don't see all near-Earth objects when approaching our planet and don't see others until they are departing."

Trenton looked solemnly at the camera, "That's a bit unnerving. This is Blake Trenton; we will continue to bring you the latest information from Russia."

March 30, 2085

12:22 PM PST

Planetary Defense Coordination Office (PDCO): The first official report of the Russian asteroid came in at 12:22 pm. The office buzzed with activity and the press clamored for a statement. While the PDCO compiled their statement about the Russian asteroid strike, another report came to the director, Jeffery Beamon, from JPL.

Another NEA (near-Earth asteroid), is approaching Earth on a similar trajectory as the Russian asteroid. It may have been a broken-off piece of the first. Three days ETA. The difference, though, is that this asteroid is nearly six times the size of the Russian asteroid and if it were to hit Earth, would destroy an area the size of half of Texas.

The director looked up with an ashen expression after reading this new report. He called his small staff of two men and two women into his office. They were expecting an update about the Russian asteroid. They got a surprise.

Once sitting at the meeting table, Beamon said, "There's another asteroid coming and it seems to be heading our way."

The two men and two women looked at Beamon's grave expression.

One woman, Linda, whispered, "Dear God."

Beamon continued, "I need a better-projected trajectory for this asteroid. I need to know if I should call the President. Could you get this for me, Linda?"

"I'm on it," Linda said, texting a message into her work pad.

A minute later, Linda said, "The trajectory is coming. They're calculating it now."

Beamon glanced at the original note and took a breath. "It's only a matter of time before one of these things hits us."

Linda's work pad vibrated, "Sir, I have the updated trajectory. It looks like a near miss. Earth will move out of its path, but it will be close. It will also just miss the Moon."

"Thank God," Beamon said under his breath.

Chapter 2

Thermopolis, Wyoming

August 8, 2085

Summer near Thermopolis, Wyoming is hot. In the distance, heat rose in rippling waves that distorted the sunbaked desert landscape. The temperature today was a blistering 97 degrees and the breeze that blew from the south gave no relief from the oppressive dry heat which seemed to suck the moisture from the air.

Professor of paleontology, Randall Wilson squinted and wiped his brow. He had hit the motherload of dinosaur remains. This may be the best find in over 90 years, he thought to himself.

They had been excavating this site for the last two months and already, more than a dozen different and complete skeletons had been unearthed and identified. There were also two skeletons of new dinosaurs, the likes of which had never been seen before. This quarry was special.

Dust blew in the rising breeze, swirling in brief vortexes that began then disappeared as they disorganized.

Professor Wilson stood with his hands on his hips, gazing over the site from a hill just above the digging and beamed with pride. He was a throwback to an era long past wearing his fedora and a button-down shirt, rolled at the sleeves, now showing signs of perspiration. He untied a small blue scarf from around his neck and wiped the sweat that had trickled down his cheek from under his hat. In his late fifties, he had a short, salt and pepper beard and round spectacles that he continually needed to clean from the constant assault of flying dust.

Bones from the ribcage of an enormous Brachiosaurus protruded from the bottom of the quarry. This beast would have been huge when it lived over a hundred million years prior in the late Jurassic period. The ribcage was so large that people stood inside its exposed half.

"Professor," came a call from one of the female interns helping to excavate the site. "You need to see this."

Professor Wilson waved and gazed up at the sun which was now past midday, then he started down the embankment slipping a bit in the loose soil. He strode up leisurely and approached several of the interns now standing with their hands on their hips and gazing blankly into the chest cavity of the half-unearthed Brachiosaurus. Though the interns sounded mystified, Professor Wilson was sure that he could handle anything that they didn't understand.

"What is it?" the Professor asked.

"We're not sure?" Deborah, one of the interns remarked questioningly.

Professor Wilson followed the intern's gaze to see, nestled next to the enormous spine, and nearly buried within the ribcage, a smooth, bronze-colored metallic object. It appeared to not be something that would exist in nature, so it shouldn't be in this place. Everything from this layer was from the late Jurassic period and nothing manufactured should be found where they now dug. This item, though, looked to have been machined and its surface as smooth as glass.

"Huh," Wilson grunted.

Deborah asked, "Should we remove this, Professor? Should we see what it is?"

She was in her late twenties and one of the brightest interns on this site. She knew the ramifications of finding something man-made amongst the bones of these dinosaurs.

"Have you photographed it yet?" the professor asked.

"Not yet."

"Okay. This is how we'll proceed. I want this fully documented. We will record the unearthing of this object. I will remove it, but each person here will give a written account of the finding."

Deborah asked, "What do you think it is, Professor?"

"I don't know, Deborah, but it shouldn't be here. I suppose it could be a hoax, but to my knowledge, this is a completely new dig site."

Professor Wilson knelt down to get a closer look at the object. He brushed at its surface. The soil around the item was hard-packed and he could tell that there wasn't but a fraction of the object showing. He could see a slight curve to its once polished surface like it could be spherical.

He cocked his head to the side and gazed at the item with a kind of wonder as one would have when his entire concept of the world might be about to change.

The Professor brought out his digging tools. He hadn't planned to dig anything on this site himself, leaving that kind of work to the interns. Then he had a shade structure erected over the metallic object, and he set out to carefully unearth it.

The day lengthened and it would soon be night. They broke for dinner and covered the new find. The professor had been painstakingly slow, using a toothbrush and attempting to find the edges of the object. The object, though metallic in color had the look of glass, so he suspected that it might be fragile. He had no intention of causing any damage to its surface.

Finishing for the day without completely unearthing the object, they walked up as a group to their campsite. There were nine tents pitched in a circle around a firepit, and smoke rose from a small crackling blaze in its center. Benches ringed the pit and as was the custom of this dig site, everyone ate on the benches and stared into the fire as the sun set.

Camp food filled their plates, beans, corn, potatoes and a cut of steak that had been grilled on a grate.

There were nineteen interns and the professor staffing this site for now. Some of the interns would come and go, while others would stay and see it through until the professor decided to pull up stakes.

They finished eating, chatting about the find.

"So, what's your best guess on that thing we found, professor?" Marcos asked.

"I'm not sure I have one. I guess if pressed, I would say that someone planted that object there. It isn't like anything that I've heard of before. There have been a couple of anomalies in the past like human footsteps preserved next to dinosaurs' footsteps in clay, but those can be explained away. I'm not sure that this can be explained if it isn't some kind of hoax."

"Maybe it's alien," Joseph exclaimed.

"Maybe you're an alien," Bill said, causing some of the interns to snicker, while a few laughed outwardly.

"I'm not kidding," he said defensively.

"Come on, Joseph," Deborah said.

Then Marcos said, "Maybe it's a dragon's egg."

Joseph bristled, "Okay, okay, shut up. It is strange, though… Geez."

Professor Wilson stared into the distance and quietly commented, speaking slowly, "It is strange."

Everyone became quiet at his tone.

The stars came out and the moonless sky darkened. There wasn't a cloud in the sky and with no lights from humanity this far out in the sticks, the constellations shone brightly above. The temperature had dropped to around seventy-five and the interns changed the direction of the discussions to movies they liked and books that they've read. They sat around the fire, gazing at the stars, then turned in for the night.

The next morning, the dig site bustled with anticipation. The hope was that the professor might lift the strange metallic object from the dirt but, though working diligently, he still hadn't reached the edges of the object.

Another day and night and the thing, whatever it was, began to take shape. The top curved downward towards the outsides of the object, and it seemed to resemble an egg, so far anyway, though probably not the dragon variety. What they could see was eight inches across and ten inches in length and smooth as polished steel.

By the middle of the day, the professor reached the artifact's curved edges and he was able to slip his gloved fingers around the top and bottom of the object. He lifted gently and to his surprise, the object popped from the hard-packed soil. It was still crusted with dirt on most of its surface, but the object was free.

A cheer rose from the interns who had stopped searching for dinosaur bones and now watched the professor with rapt attention.

The artifact was nearly egg-shaped, but more symmetrical and appeared to be made of some kind of metal. It was surprisingly light which made the professor think that it was hollow.

The object was nearly a foot in length and ten inches across. Its surface, the parts that were clean, were a metallic color close to a dull bronze, but not exactly. When the sun glinted off of it, the artifact was more the color of pewter and seemed to have some kind of clear coat which made the color appear to float beneath its surface.

Professor Wilson looked up through his spectacles at the interns and smiled then carried the object from the quarry. A kind of solemn procession followed him as he proceeded through the dirt paths and to a specific tent that was larger than the ones that housed the interns.

This tent was erected for special finds. Reaching the entrance, he nodded at Deborah to open the tent flap. He didn't want to take either hand from the strange object.

She pulled the flap aside and he entered followed by everyone who worked at the dig. This tent was quite large but the group of nineteen workers filled most of the free space where there weren't tables strewn with bones.

The Professor carried the egg-shaped artifact to a table in the middle and set it down in its center. He stepped back and rubbed his hands unconsciously on his pants gawking at something that defied explanation. Everyone else stood silently waiting for some word from the Professor, but he just stared.

He looked around as if just noticing that the tent was filled with people.

He nervously said, "Well, what do you say that I clean this up a bit?"

The group returned a nervous and subdued laugh.

Professor Wilson approached the object carefully and began to remove portions of caked dirt from its surface. In the space of an hour, he had freed it from all but a layer of dust clinging to it. He hesitated, contemplating whether or not to use water on the odd metal. He didn't want to damage it.

Deciding, he said, "Bring me some water and a soft towel, please."

He considered that it had been exposed to water for millennia and couldn't see the harm. It wasn't as if it was found in a cave, protected from the elements. Besides, he was curious as to how the peculiar surface would look once cleaned.

He focused a bright lamp onto the egg and began bathing it gently as one might bathe an infant. Within minutes, the egg-shaped object was cleaned. He stood back and gazed around at the interns, who hadn't appeared to even breathe during the process.

The light glistened off the egg's glass-like surface.

The Professor said, "Well, now what do you think? Any speculations?"

Deborah said, "It's an anomaly. I've never believed in aliens before, but this shouldn't have been found where we found it and it didn't appear to have been placed there. If this is a hoax, it's a well-played one."

The professor said, "I couldn't have said it better. Anyone else?"

The rest of the interns stood silently.

"I'm going to need to drive this to the university tonight. I can't leave it out here. Take a good look, this might be the last time you ever see it."

Some students held out their cell phones to get a quick picture. Most just stood and stared.

Just then, light began to undulate just under the surface of the egg as if drawing power from somewhere. Tiny sparks of what looked like fireworks exploded then disappeared beneath the clearcoat of its shell.

The professor stepped back a step and so did everyone else. An aurora of twisting and folding light began to squirm just under the egg's skin, then, where the fireworks had been. Just as suddenly as it began, the light show stopped and the object became quiet.

The professor stepped forward to get a closer look and the entire room seemed to lean with him.

The object then began to faintly glow and the very top layer of its surface seemed to become more translucent. Everyone stepped back, again.

From the top portion of the bronze artifact, white light began to emerge as if peeking from it like a prairie dog from its burrow. Then the light increased, reaching outward, towards the top of the tent. The light then changed separating into columns of blue and green. At first, the light seemed to move randomly like the lights of a hundred searchlights shining into the sky, but then they slowed to a stop and a type of hologram appeared just above the surface of the egg. Within the hologram, you could see depth and width as streams of individual columns of blue and green pointed up while others connected those same lines with right angles in three-dimensional grids.

Inside the green columns, short, black lines began to slowly creep from near the egg's surface. Some were pointing straight upward while others were at an angle like backslashes on a computer keyboard. They glided upward within the green grids in the holographic display. Up they traveled until some began to enter the side green columns that connected to the adjacent horizontal green columns. Here, the black lines then joined the procession of the black lines in the upward columns. To this point, the blue columns of light remained empty, but then they began to fill.

It was now an orderly jumble of short, black, straight lines, both vertical and backslash moving through the blue and green columns, traversing their pathways.

Several of the interns gasped.

Marcos said, "What the hell?"

"Indeed," the professor agreed, gawking at the sight, and trying to make sense of something that made no sense. He needed to step back further to get a better look at the holographic display. It shined nearly four feet above the egg which was acting as its projector. The lines were now streaming from the object as if trying to convey a message of some kind. The professor reached over and turned off the light so that he could better see the display, but as the light extinguished, the egg seemed to power down and the hologram dimmed. Within five minutes, the hologram disappeared and the egg became dormant once more.

Wilson said, "Marcos, get the jeep ready, we're leaving right now."

Professor Wilson wrapped the egg in a red and green, plaid blanket that had been jumbled in a corner of the tent and carried it out to the now running jeep. Then he and Marcos were off in a cloud of dust.

They drove the metallic egg to the University of Wyoming, where, by this time, night had begun to fall and lights were on all over the campus. They drove directly to Professor Wilson's building and they parked and carried the egg to his office.

Entering, Professor Wilson set the egg on his desk. His office was orderly with a full bookshelf and several filing cabinets. There were two glass cases with bones that had cards under each with descriptions of the bones.

Marcos looked directly at the professor. He asked, "What now?"

"I have a friend in the physics department. I think I'll call him. He's usually here late."

"Should I go?" Marcos asked.

"Yes. I'll stay with the egg tonight and find out what to do with it tomorrow. I'm not sure how to proceed." Then Wilson confessed, "I'm not sure what we have here."

"I think Joseph was right. I think that this is alien technology. The government is going to want it, and I mean yesterday."

The professor thought about that and a bit of paranoia crept into the edges of his mind. "I think we need to keep this very quiet for now. I think you should go."

Marcos nodded and said, "I think I should go, too. This suddenly feels dangerous."

"Marcos, go back to the dig and suggest that the interns keep this quiet also."

"Okay, but I could see some of them posting to their social media accounts as we left."

"I was afraid of that."

Wilson nodded and picked up the phone.

As Marcos walked to the door, he turned and said, "Be careful, Professor." He then walked out, closing the door quietly.

Wilson dialed his friend's cell phone. His friend answered, "Hello."

"Jamal, are you still at the college?"

"Hi, Randall, yes, I was just heading out. Aren't you in the field at your bone Shangri-La?"

Wilson smiled to himself. "I just came back. I have something that I want you to see. I need some advice."

"I'll swing by on my way. Be there in about five minutes."

Professor Jamal Irving, P.H.D. was the top physicist in the Physics department at the university. He reached Wilson's office, tapped on the door then walked in. Doctor Irving was not tall, maybe five-ten, African American with an infectious smile. Like Wilson, he was in his late fifties. He and Professor Wilson had been good friends for at least ten years.

As he entered, he could see the look of concern on Wilson's face.

"What is it, Randall?" he said, closing the door.

Professor Wilson took a deep breath and pulled the blanket off of the metallic egg. It glistened under the low light of the office.

Doctor Irving said, "That's interesting. So?"

"We found this buried with a hundred-million-year-old dinosaur skeleton, an undisturbed skeleton."

"I'm not a paleontologist, but that doesn't seem possible."

"It's not, naturally. This is manmade."

Doctor Irving nodded knowingly. "And no humans, to our knowledge, were around back then?"

Wilson solemnly nodded and said, "That's correct."

"Huh?"

"Indeed."

"Could it be some kind of prank?"

"Honestly, I would say, not a chance."

"Huh?" A pause, then, "Are you sure?"

Professor Wilson nodded and placed the item directly under his desk lamp. Light glistened off the egg's surface then the egg, just as before, came to life with the firework display first sparking below its surface and then the twisting, writhing aurora began, followed by the hologram which sprung forth with its columns of vertical and slanted lines.

"Oh shit!" Doctor Irving exclaimed.

Wilson pulled the light away and after a few silent minutes, the hologram winked out. Doctor Irving stared at the sight with his eyes wide and his mouth slightly open.

He looked at Wilson and said, "Well, that was something."

"And not from this planet?" Wilson suggested questioningly.

"Not anything that I have ever heard of."

"What do I do, now?"

Irving breathed out forcefully. "I hesitate to say this, but I think you need to give it to the big heads in the government. It goes against my grain, but I think that's information being broadcasted in that hologram, though maybe alien, and as imperfect as our government is, I don't think I would want it to land in the hands of our enemies, of which we have many."

"You were military, right?"

"Yeah, Navy. I was a pilot for some years."

"Who do we take this to?"

Doctor Irving shook his head. "Don't know off the top of my head. Let me make a couple of calls."

"I'm afraid to even have this thing right now. I feel like Frodo from 'The Lord of the Rings.' Can I bring it to your house, tonight, and you can come with me to bring it somewhere in the morning?"

"I don't know if that's the best idea. I think you should go to a hotel somewhere and call me in the morning. Disappear, you know. How many other people know about this?"

"At least the nineteen interns at the dig site."

"That means that it will be all over social media before long, probably already is."

"Yeah?"

"So, that means that all of our enemies probably know something about it and where it's going."

"Oh," Professor Wilson said with some despair. "Is there someplace we can lock it here?"

"No place safe that I can think of."

"Okay," Wilson said making a decision. "Me and this egg-thing are going to disappear for the night. I'll call you first thing in the morning. Please have some place where I can get rid of it."

"I'm on it, Randall. You get lost and call me first thing."

Chapter 3

The door closed and professor Wilson was on his own. Where to go? No time to plan, he just had to leave. The first thing that he did was to turn off his cell phone and pull the battery. He contemplated leaving it altogether, but if it was off, with no battery, no one should be able to track him… Or could they? He didn't think so.

Where to go?

He pulled a green gym bag from the bottom drawer of his desk, one used to go to his light workout in the University gym and put the blanket wrapped egg into it. He had to leave. What about his car? Someone could track him by his car… All cars now had GPS built into their digital displays. What to do? Most people now used automated cars that took you to your location.

What about his credit cards? They all had radio frequency chips in them to help prevent fraud. He'd leave the cards in his office, but he might need cash. He needed to bring his ATM card. He had a cover for it that blocked the chip.

He walked from his office carrying the bag and locked the door, looked up and down the long hallway that led to and from the teachers' offices, and strode down the hall to where his car was parked.

Unmarried, he had no worries at home, except for his cat, who would be fine. His neighbor had been feeding it every morning since he started the dig. He had eleven hours to kill until he would be able to connect with Jamal.

As he neared the doors into the parking lot, he ran into Marjorie Whitcome. She had been a light friend for a couple of years, a math teacher and also unmarried. He hustled to catch up.

"Hi, Marjorie," Wilson called as he jogged to reach her.

"Oh, Randall. I haven't seen you for a bit."

"Yes. I've been working in the field at a dig site near Thermopolis."

"Oh, so, how's that going?"

"Great. Ah… Can I ask you a favor?"

"Sure."

"My car is having some trouble and I'm supposed to meet a friend at the movies, downtown. Is there any chance that you could drop me close to there? Might it be on your way home?"

"It's close to where I live. Sure, I'd be happy to. My ride should be waiting."

"Thank you so much."

They walked together out into the parking lot and waiting at the curb was a white football-shaped vehicle the size of a van. Its side door slid open.

They stepped into an automated car with no driver and Marjorie said, "Swing me past downtown please."

"Yes Ma'am," a male voice said from a speaker in the front of the vehicle. "Please place your hand on the verification pad."

She reached over and placed her hand on a pad which lit green and then she and the Professor sat down in the seats in the rear of the car. The door slid closed.

"Please buckle your seatbelts," the male voice said.

They did as requested and Wilson set the bag on the floor.

He had no plan, but he knew that the last movie was a 10:00 or 10:30 start time and would get him out around 1:00 AM. He would use those three hours to come up with some kind of plan and around eight hours to kill until he reconnected with his friend, Jamal, who he hoped would come up with someone to give this technology to.

Marjorie's ride took him the several blocks towards the theater, while she made small talk that he barely heard. He noticed a bus station a block off the main street and that gave him an idea.

When they stopped at an intersection, Wilson said, "Let me out here please." The car pulled to the curb and the door slid open. He said, "Thank you so much, Marjorie. I owe you one."

She blinked a bit blankly and nodded, saying, "We haven't arrived at the theater yet."

"I know, but this will do. Thanks again."

The door closed and he was off. He held the bag close to himself, hugging it like his life savings were inside and once realizing that, he dropped it to his side and carried it like the gym bag that it was.

Wilson jogged back towards the Greyhound bus station. He passed a stand-alone ATM and took $600 out of the machine and then headed off, looking warily over his shoulder. No one could be following, but his imagination was in overdrive and his paranoia growing.

Arriving at the station, he walked through the double doors. The station had an austere waiting room with several rows of plastic chairs and against one wall, rows of vending machines that had everything from candy to paperback novels.

A young man walked to one of the machines with the novels and pushed a button, then waved his watch over a pay pad and the book dropped into a tray with a thump.

Professor Wilson walked to a window with an older, balding man sitting behind bulletproof glass at a small counter.

"Yes?" the man said pleasantly.

"How much for a ticket to Cheyenne?"

The man glanced at a small flat computer screen and said, "Two hundred and ninety-nine bucks."

Wilson asked, "What time does the bus leave?"

"It will arrive here in about an hour and will depart fifteen minutes later."

Wilson nodded and purchased for cash, a one-way ticket to Cheyenne. He turned and glanced at the nearly deserted waiting room and felt temporarily safe.

He walked to the hard, plastic seats provided by the station, sat and dozed with the bag on his lap and the straps wrapped around his arms. He woke startled after a half-hour nap, glancing quickly up at a clock on the wall above the ticket window. As he sat, his paranoia continued to grow. He watched the clock as the second hand ticked off the seconds and he hoped that the bus wouldn't be late.

By the time the bus arrived, an hour had passed just as the man had said. Wilson's nerves were on the rise and he began to sweat. He boarded the bus and started out to Cheyenne, feeling some relief from being on the bus, but he knew that it was only temporary.

People were going to want this thing, people would probably be willing to kill to get it. It wasn't going to take long for word of it to get out and spread like a fire in a dried grassy field.

The bus arrived at the station in Cheyenne and Wilson stepped off. He walked into the waiting room and it appeared to be a carbon copy of the first. He needed to think, and he sat for a time, not sure what to do next, but he felt that he couldn't have been followed here. Then he thought that he might be able to find a motel room for the night paying cash. Most wouldn't give him a room without identification but he hoped to bribe someone at a motel desk and give them a lame story.

He walked from the bus station and down a busy street until he came upon several motels in a row. He walked into the office of the first one. It was small, had a two-person faux-leather couch with a slight rip in the seat and a desk with a lamp throwing dull light into the room. Wilson approached the desk. A man in his late forties watched as he approached.

"Hello," Professor Wilson said.

"Hello," the man behind the counter replied.

"I, ah, have a problem. I've lost my wallet and phone and need a place to sleep for the night. I have some cash but don't know if it will be enough for a room. Could you tell me your rates?"

"We don't rent out rooms to anyone without identification."

"I figured that and I can pay you upfront. I'm just passing through on my way to Laramie and was hoping for a room. I live there, you see and can't get a connecting bus until tomorrow. If you would be so kind to make an exception, I would greatly appreciate it. I'm frankly beat."

The guy looked at him then glanced behind Wilson. "You alone?"

"Yes."

"No woman?"

"No," Wilson said perplexed. Then he realized that the insinuation was that he had a prostitute waiting. "No," Wilson repeated a bit more forcefully and shaking his head. "I just need some sleep."

The guy behind the desk gave Wilson a sideways glance.

Wilson could tell that the guy thought that at least half of the story was bull, but then he nodded.

"I guess I can't make you sleep on the street."

"Oh, thank you, sir."

"That'll be two hundred and fifty dollars. It includes a non-refundable deposit."

Professor Wilson nodded and paid the man who made Wilson fill out paperwork asking his name and address.

Professor Wilson lied of course. By this time, he didn't need to tell the truth.

The man gave him two key cards and said, "Check out time is 11:00 AM."

Wilson walked from the office and found the room. It was austere, painted a dull light brown with a double bed, no TV, a small dresser, and a nightstand. It depressed him just to walk inside, but he could feel the air go out of his sails and all he could think of was laying down. He let the door close then set the bag holding the artifact on the floor by the bed. He laid down, exhausted and quickly fell asleep in all his clothes.

Professor Wilson woke with a start, disoriented. Where was he? He could see the sun streaming into his room through a gap in the drab, brown drapes. What time was it? He glanced around for a clock. 9:45 AM... Late... He needed to call his friend, but not from here. He needed to find a park where he could see at least several escape routes. He felt drained... How do spies do it? How do they keep up their strength? He had only been at this for one night and he had already had enough.

He slowly sat up and draped his legs over the side of the bed trying to clear the cobwebs. He checked to see that the bag with the egg was where he left it then reluctantly pushed himself to standing and shuffled into the bathroom. He washed his face, grabbed the bag and left the room dropping the key cards on a table by the window. Before closing the door, he glanced back. Because he had fallen asleep on top of the bed, the room didn't appear to have been slept in at all. He let the door shut and looked down at his rumpled clothes. He hadn't changed them in two days and sleeping in them did them no good. He felt a mess and tried to push several wrinkles out with his hands. It was hopeless. He shrugged and walked out into a bright day that was going to be hot.

Hungry, and with fifty bucks remaining, he walked to a diner just down the road and ordered a three-egg omelet with home fries and coffee. He thought about his situation and felt a shudder. If this egg-thing was truly alien, he would be the most sought-after man on Earth.

Finishing breakfast, he walked out into the sunny day to hopefully find a park or some kind of recreational area with which to blend into and disappear. As he walked, he came upon Frontier Mall. He smiled and thought, next best thing to a park.

As he entered the mall, he pulled out his cell phone, stuck the battery inside the back and turned it on. Once it came up, he quickly called Jamal.

"Hey," Jamal said. "I was getting worried about you."

"I felt like I had to find a safe place to call you from."

Jamal became serious and said, "Your office was broken into last night."

"Damn."

"And your house."

"Oh," Wilson said with growing fear. "Have you found someone who I can give this thing to?"

"Yeah. I have an old Navy buddy who's now a field agent for the F.B.I. I gave him a vague outline of the story and asked him to meet me today. He should be here in a couple of hours. Where are you? Do you feel safe where you are?"

"I don't feel safe anywhere."

"Okay. Call me back at 11:00 and we'll figure out a place to meet. Do you have the item with you?"

"Of course."

"Good."

"Talk to you later."

Professor Wilson hung up and turned back off his phone. He couldn't contain his paranoia. Everywhere he looked, he saw potential foreign agents. He had to leave. He decided to walk the length of the mall and exit out the other side. He thought that maybe he would find an overpass to sit under until he called his friend back.

Wilson came to a Dillard's department store, walked through the clothing section and found a door to the parking lot.

When he exited, he was grabbed by six men dressed in black jumpsuits, four with assault rifles and they ushered him to a helicopter that was also black, parked haphazardly in the parking lot. Wilson was shocked and wanted to resist but the men were forceful.

"You're coming with us, Sir," one of the black-clad men commanded.

Wilson didn't speak.

The blades of the copter were already spinning and they pushed the air down forcefully against the parking lot throwing dust and litter away from the craft. The next thing Wilson knew, he was in the air. One of the men opened the gym bag, peeked in and closed it again.

Wilson said, "I hope you work for the United States."

"We do, sir."

Professor Wilson breathed a sigh of relief.

Thirty minutes later, the helicopter touched down in a remote region of Wyoming. The side door slid open and Wilson looked outside to see another helicopter waiting with blades spinning.

There had been little discussion. The man sitting by the bag which contained the egg said to Wilson, "Sir, would you please go to that helicopter? It will take you and this," he pointed at the bag, "to your destination."

Wilson stood and stepped out of the helicopter that he arrived in. Another man carried the bag with the egg and they proceeded to his next ride. The rotating blades of both copters threw dust high into the air.

Standing under the spinning blades of the next copter were two men wearing dark suits, sunglasses, and thin ties. They waited as Wilson and the other man approached.

"Hello, professor," the first said loudly.

Professor Wilson nodded.

"My name is James Bennet. I work for the N.S.A. We are very glad to have found you first. I would like to bring you to a base that is kept fairly secret. I wish to debrief you about your find. Because you found it in your best interest to disappear, I'm sure you know how important your find may be. Would you accompany me, sir?".

"Yes, of course, Mister Bennet."

"Thank you, sir."

They walked several steps to a waiting helicopter. It didn't look military. It had more the appearance of one that might be used by the State Department to carry dignitaries. They lifted off and left for parts unknown. Professor Wilson was positioned so he couldn't see out of the windows and after an hour's flight, they touched down.

He was led with his gym bag to a building that had no markings. It was grey and boxlike with a tiled roof and set in a small fenced-in compound, nestled in a narrow valley and was surrounded by several other buildings with the same look. The weather felt much the same as the stifling Wyoming heat that he had experienced for the last few days, hot and dry.

Wilson was ushered into the first building, through an austere hallway and into an office that had no identification on the door. The man, Mister Bennet, accompanied him carrying the gym bag.

The office had no secretary and once inside, Mister Bennet pushed a button by another unmarked door. The door opened and Bennet waved Wilson inside.

Another man in a suit, short and unassuming, with thick glasses and a military haircut sat behind a small desk in a room with little furnishings. There were several chairs that surrounded a meeting table, a large TV screen, and no windows to the outside world.

The man stood when Professor Wilson walked in. He stepped around his desk and offered his hand. Bennet handed the gym bag to the man and walked out of the office.

"Hello, Professor. I'm glad to see you. My name is George Sanderson. I'm anxious to see what you have found." He paused for a minute then said, "I think it's a game-changer. I'm glad that we got to you first. I know of several foreign governments that had already sent agents to find you."

"I heard that someone broke into my office and my home," Wilson said a bit shaken.

"Well, that was us. We were in a hurry."

"Am I under arrest. I get the feeling that I might just disappear. Should I be worried?"

"No, Professor. This is so much bigger than that. You don't realize this, but word of your discovery has already traversed the globe. Because of social media, your interns have let all the world know of your find. We just want to talk to you and get the exact story of how you found this, "thing," and what you've discovered about it."

Professor Wilson outlined the story from start to finish. He then explained that he felt that the egg was powered by placing a light close to its surface. He said that he thought that it somehow absorbed the energy from the light and used it to light its holographic display.

Mister Sanderson took the egg from the gym bag, unwrapped it from the blanket and brought it to the table. He stood back with almost the reverence of someone approaching a holy relic.

He breathed out, then said, "Show me?"

Professor Wilson moved the artifact directly under Sanderson's desk lamp and turned it on.

Sanderson watched and for the first few minutes, nothing happened. He looked questioningly at Wilson who just shrugged, then the light show began under the egg's surface. Fireworks of color streaked the egg's facade, then an aroura squirmed and wriggled where the fireworks had ceased. Last, the aurora stopped and the egg faintly glowed.

Sanderson watched with his mouth slightly agape and his eyes wide.

Next, lights issued from the egg and the hologram appeared with the grids of blue and green, then the horizontal lines and slashes.

"I'll be damned," Sanderson said.

Professor Wilson asked, "So, does this put us centuries ahead of the world technologically?"

"It would, Professor if we didn't plan to share it. If it's really alien, it's too big for us to claim as our own. It makes the world far too dangerous for us because our enemies and our allies will become too paranoid. We're thinking that we will have to share it because if we don't, we're afraid that the world might destabilize. We'll try to decipher it first, or at least try to record it to see if we can find some patterns, but we won't wait too long to share it. We are probably going to put together a small team of scientists from several countries to study it first."

Professor Wilson nodded, then considered Sanderson's words. One thing was for sure, the world had just changed forever.

"We have a request of you, Professor, to buy us a bit of time. We would like you, once you leave here, to say that we think that it's a hoax. We figure that will buy us several weeks to maybe a couple of months. We just don't want some of our enemies to come up with a solution to this code before we do, one that they might not be willing to share."

"I think I understand," Wilson said, now beginning to sense the gravity of the situation. "Can I leave?"

"Yes, we'll get you home... Oh, mind if I keep the bag and blanket?"

"No problem," the Professor said, "That's fine."

Chapter 4

Fifteen minutes from the time Professor Wilson had walked into Sanderson's office, he left for the helicopter to take him away. He couldn't express the relief of not having the egg-thing with him. Though he was correct in some of his speculations of the danger of having it, he hadn't fully comprehended. Had he met the wrong people while he had the egg, he would now, probably, be dead. He felt a shudder go through his body as the helicopter lifted off, but it wasn't from the machine, it was from now realized fear.

An hour passed and the helicopter touched down at a small airport, Cheyenne Regional, designed for small private planes. The blades of the helicopter continued to spin as Wilson was ushered from a large open door on the side.

The man who ushered him away from the helicopter said loudly, "Sir, we have a car for you to take you anywhere you choose. Where can we drop you, Sir?"

"Take me back to the college. My car is there. I need it to get home."

"Yes, Sir," the man, obviously military, said formally.

Wilson was shown to a black sedan with government plates and driven from the airport. Twenty-five minutes later, he was back at the college. He stepped from the car and stretched, looked around and walked into his building. When he got to his office, it was in some disarray, but not treated disrespectfully. He hoped his home would be similar, but he doubted that. He picked up his office phone and dialed Jamal.

"Hello," Jamal said answering.

"Hey, buddy," Wilson said.

"Randall, boy am I glad to hear your voice. I was worried."

"Yeah. I got snatched by the N.S.A. Don't ever think that you can stay away from those guys if they're looking for you."

Jamal paused, then said, "I'm on my way down. I don't want to talk on the phone." He hung up and two minutes later, opened Professor Wilson's door.

Wilson was tidying up from the search and glanced up and smiled.

"So, did they use cattle prods where the sun don't shine?" Jamal said grinning.

"No, they were very polite."

"Oh. That's interesting."

"Yep."

"Did they take the egg?"

"Yep."

"What did they say about it?"

"I can't say right now."

"Wooh. I know what that means."

"You're the military guy."

"Will I ever be able to hear your story?"

"Yeah, and I think pretty soon, just not right now."

"Damn, I think I know what that means, also."

"You're one of the smartest guys I know, Jamal," Wilson said sincerely.

August 11, 2085

Word of the egg-like object traveled like wildfire. The University of Wyoming, where Professor Wilson worked, began being contacted by several news stations including CNN and Fox News. The next day, several news trucks camped out in front of Professor Wilson's home and as he walked out for work in the morning, he was approached by a dozen news people and their camera crews.

All the news people began speaking at once.

"Professor! Is it true!?" a lady dressed business-like, with blond hair that didn't move in the breeze, asked excitedly.

Wilson didn't respond.

A man in a suit and tie asked next, "Tell us what you've found, Professor. Do you think it's alien?"

They stopped Wilson, standing in front of him, and not allowing him to reach his car. He had no choice but to answer.

"I've taken the object that you're talking about to the government. They are looking at it, but they told me that they think it's a well-played prank. It fooled us at the dig site though, so we got it to the authorities."

"Professor, we've all seen some video from the site of it flashing some kind of lights, but the images were grainy."

"It did do that, but we didn't tell anyone at the dig to keep it secret because we suspected that it might have been some kind of hoax. If we thought, for sure, that it was a real alien artifact, we would have, of course, told the interns on the dig to keep it secret, and they would have done so."

"What do you really think of the artifact, Professor?" another news reporter shouted.

"I think it's probably some kind of hoax like the government said. We've been digging up dinosaur bones for more than a hundred years and not found anything that would lead anyone to suspect that we had been visited by aliens. There are other interesting artifacts, though, cave paintings and the like, where you might read into them of some alien visitation, but nothing from a hundred-million-years ago. I think it's safe to say, that it's someone putting something over on us."

Disappointment showed on the faces of some of the news people.

Wilson said, "Now, can I get to work, please?"

The news people parted and Wilson got into his car, breathing a sigh of relief.

He drove to the college, where he was called to the administration building, and he gave the same story. Leaving there, he hoped that the attention around him would die down so he could get back to digging up dinosaur bones. In the back of his mind, though, he knew that very soon, the world would find out that this was no hoax. He also suspected that the lines and slashes would be deciphered just like the aliens, who placed the egg-shaped artifact on Earth had known would happen, once we had the technology to do so.

Chapter 5

Edwards Air Force Facility, Nevada.

Area 51

August 13, 2085

The reputation of this remote detachment of Edwards Air Force Base is well known. It's a dusty wasteland in a dry lakebed and home to the infamous Area 51, the United States' link to everything extraterrestrial where vast conspiracy theories abound to this day, most associated with UFOs.

One reality is for certain, that it has been the continual home to secret testing of many different types of top-secret weapons and aircraft.

0825 Hours PST

By a helicopter pad at Edwards Air Force Base, three men, two in uniform and one in a business suit, waited in sunglasses with expressions of anticipation.

The sound of large helicopter blades slapping the air rose from the north, then three jet fighters buzzed the airfield.

The three men turned to see the large blue and white Boeing, dual bladed helicopter approach the landing pad.

The three stealth fighters finished another pass and disappeared in the distance. Then, escorted by three next-generation Apache Attack Helicopters, the Boeing copter approached and set down on the landing pad. The Apaches waited for several heartbeats, then pulled away to vanish as dust rose from the slowing Boeing's blades. As the copter's blades slowed further, the large side door slid open.

George Sanderson, dressed in suit and tie, stepped from the helicopter carrying an unremarkable, green, common gym bag. He ducked slightly, reflexively avoiding the circling blades that hovered several feet above his head and stirred the dust. He walked briskly to the three men awaiting his arrival, stopped, held out his free hand and said, "Hello, General Matthews. Good to see you again, Sir."

"Hi, George," General Matthews said, "This is Lieutenant Colonel Portis, who will be in charge of security and Professor Sing, who will head up the science teams."

Portis was African American with a stern expression. His hat sat forward and his posture at a constant state of attention. Doctor Sing had more the look of a family doctor. He was Asian and dressed casually in his fifties with thick salt and pepper hair parted on the side and dark-rimmed glasses with tinted lenses.

Sanderson shook each's hand.

"Gentlemen, this is George Sanderson."

Once finished with the introductions, Matthews said, "Let's get this, "*thing*," inside and take a look at it."

The four men walked towards a black limousine with two serious men standing on each side. As they approached, the man on the driver's side opened the back door and the four men stepped inside. They sat and the limo started off.

The General said, "George, I can't tell you how excited I am to see this thing."

Sanderson said, "It's like nothing that I've ever seen before."

"So, you think it's genuine?"

"No doubt in my mind."

They drove a short distance to a building that had the appearance of a hardened bunker. The driveway to the building sloped downward as most of the building did not protrude far from above the ground. The door of the building slid open slowly to its left. It had the appearance of a vault door, thick and impenetrable. Once it had fully opened, the limo drove inside and stopped. The large vault door then slid closed. Six armed soldiers stood at attention inside the vault, all with assault rifles.

The men inside the limo stepped from it and General Matthews said, "This way, gentlemen."

The four men, Sanderson, Portis, Sing, and Matthews, walked to an elevator which was the only door available to them after entering the vault.

General Matthews placed his hand on an identification pad, followed by each of the other men. The door wouldn't open to anyone who wasn't authorized and didn't have prior permission to enter. The elevator doors slid open. Once inside, the elevator descended rapidly.

Sanderson continued to carry the bag with the egg. No one spoke until the elevator stopped and the door opened into a white hallway with several doors on each side.

"My office is this way," the General stated.

He walked the four men down the hallway and into his outer office. This was not standard procedure. No one was quite sure if this artifact was real. No one wanted to take the blame if it wasn't, so, it fell upon General Matthews and Doctor Sing to decide whether or not to proceed. If they thought that this was a hoax, they wouldn't study it. If they thought it might be a hoax, the thing would be locked in a secret place just in case they were wrong. If they determined that this might be real, then the artifact would begin the process of being thoroughly studied and a team of scientists, that Sanderson was initially told about, would probably be assembled. But the United States government did not want the world to know that they had been fooled by a hoax.

Matthews instructed Portis to wait in the outer office, then said to Sing and Sanderson, "Follow me, please."

He led them into his austere office with a desk, several chairs, and a meeting table.

General Matthews said, "Please sit, gentlemen."

The General sat behind his desk and the other two men sat in chairs before it. He paused contemplatively, looking at each face across from him then began, "Gentlemen, we have a decision to make. The problem that we face is that we don't want to waste our time on something that might be a fake. I'm hoping that after today, we will be able to go ahead with some study or decide that a good joke has been played on the Professor at the dig site and us. If so, we can all have a good laugh, find out who did this, and have them locked up for the rest of their lives. Now, George, tell us what you know."

"Yes, Sir. I have seen this thing in action. My opinion is that this is no hoax."

"Okay, show us."

Sanderson said, "As you probably know, this was found amongst undisturbed dinosaur bones. The professor who found it said that it shouldn't have been there."

Both Sing and Matthews nodded.

Sanderson removed the egg from the gym bag and placed it beneath the General's desk lamp. "Turn on the lamp, Sir."

The General nodded and switched on the lamp. For the space of about three minutes, nothing happened. The egg just sat. Then, without warning, the fireworks began just under its clear-coat surface. Color bursts like expanding flowers spread out and seemed to connect other color bursts which seemed to ignite still others.

The men watched with flat expressions.

The fireworks increased and picked up in intensity.

"Is this what you saw before?" the General asked Sanderson.

"Yes, Sir, and more."

Next, the aurora began as the fireworks decreased. It wriggled and squirmed over the surface of the egg with undulating colors of green, blue and white. Matthews watched with a flat expression and he glanced at Sanderson who also watched. Doctor Sing's eyes couldn't be opened any wider.

Doctor Sing said, "I heard about this but seeing it is a whole different thing. It's stranger than I expected."

The egg began to glow as the aurora ceased, then a white light poked out from the top of the surface. The light was odd and seemed self-contained, illuminating nothing around it. It flickered, emerging from the surface, then receded only to emerge again, playing a kind of peek-a-boo.

The room was silent.

White light shot out towards the ceiling but stopped short of it. It should have lit the ceiling but didn't. It divided into many different streams of light, then each turned to green and blue. This led to the holographic image as the streams of light seemed to make dimensions and angles in what now appeared as some kind of field. Short vertical lines and backslashes began to slowly crawl up the green streams of light, they then bent, some moving to the right, some to the left, some backward, connecting with other streams of lines and slashes. Next, the blue columns began to fill with the backslashes and vertical lines.

"Damn," Doctor Sing whispered. "What the hell is this thing?"

"Something not from this planet," General Matthews stated flatly.

No one blinked. They watched silently as the holographic grid streamed up and outward. No one moved.

The General smiled, "Well, Doctor Sing, worth studying?"

"I don't know what to say. I can't wait to get started."

Matthews said, "I'll lock it up for now and in the morning, we'll walk it down to Lab 126a." He paused looking at the egg, and then continued, "How do we turn it off?"

Sanderson said, "Just turn off the light. It doesn't seem to be activated with overhead lights. It seems to need the light to be closer."

The General turned off his desk lamp and after a minute, the hologram began to fade.

General Matthews said, "What do you think, Doctor Sing? Could this be as obvious as it seems?"

"To be honest, I think so. If I were going to guess, I'd say it was some kind of code, like binary."

"Do you think we could decipher it?"

"I don't know. All the languages that we know of have some similarities. Since we all agree that this isn't from this planet, it will take some time to find some kind of common thread to understand it. I don't think that something placed with a dinosaur a hundred-million years ago spoke the Queen's English. But, I don't think it will take long to find out. I think if we film the code and put it through our supercomputers, we'll get an answer pretty quick, at least to the fact that it might be some kind of communication. I'm not sure where that will lead us, though. It might be too advanced, or just too alien for us, like trying to understand an earthworm. I just don't know."

"Tomorrow, we'll get it to the lab," Matthews said. "George, you can leave."

Sanderson nodded.

They all stood and walked from the office.

Chapter 6

Office of the President of the United States.

August 12, 2085

2:20 PM EDT

Chief of Staff, Howard Diamond: "Sir, we have been fielding calls all day from nearly every country in the U.N. Security Council. They want to know about the egg."

"I figured that would happen," President Dent said. "I'll begin returning the calls starting with China, then Russia, then Great Britain and last Germany. You handle the rest."

"And I tell them that we think the egg is a fake?"

"That's what we say as convincingly as we can."

"We've had more than the normal attempts to breach our data security in the last two days."

"No surprise there. I want you to make sure that there is no data coming out of that lab, not a flash drive or laptop or pad, not even a cell phone. I want everything completely locked down and the only way I want any information to come out of there is by you going there personally and bringing the information to me and whispering it into my ear. No slip-ups. I'm holding you responsible."

"I've already connected with Colonel Portis who is in charge of security and have outlined everything to him. He assures me that not a single word will leave the lab."

"That's what I want to hear, now let's get to lying to the rest of the world."

Two hours of spin and outright falsehood later, President Dent and Howard Diamond finished assuring every country on the U.N. Security Council that the egg was a well-conceived hoax and that an investigation as to who were the perpetrators, was underway. The world wasn't convinced, though, but they had no information to suggest otherwise.

Professor Wilson was also informed that the egg was a hoax and that once checked out in the lab, the trick of the hologram was uncovered. Wilson wasn't so sure, but it wasn't his problem anymore and he was glad for it. Everything around the egg-thing felt dangerous, like knowing a secret against some Mafia crime boss who knew you knew. Thankfully it was out of his hands.

Chapter 7

Edwards Air Force Base

Lab 126a

August 14, 2085.

10:10 AM PDT

The egg arrived at lab 126a inconspicuously in its austere gym bag, wrapped in a blanket, carried by General Matthews and accompanied by Doctor Sing and Lieutenant Colonel Portis. As they entered the lab area, several people dressed in white lab coats looked up surprised to see the three men. Doctor Sing was there, from time to time, but Portis and Matthews were not and Matthews was a big shot. Something was up.

The lab workers watched as Doctor Sing led General Matthews towards a private portion of the lab where they stopped at an unmarked door. No one who worked there had been in this portion of the lab before. Portis waited in the forward portion of the lab which looked onto several glass-enclosed rooms. Each had several banks of computer workstations set up to observe each room.

Doctor Sing said, "Marriam and Sanjay, could you come with us, please?"

Now everyone had stopped their work and were looking on. Marriam and Sanjay glanced at each other questioningly, then stepped after General Matthews and Doctor Sing.

Doctor Sing led them through the unmarked door into a short hallway, and to a security door which he opened with a keypad and thumbprint, then down another short hallway. Sing opened another unmarked door with his handprint and retina scan. The four entered an empty room with no other doors and no windows.

Marriam and Sanjay gazed around. Their first worry was that they had done something wrong but couldn't understand what. Then looking around, both simultaneously thought, what could they do in this room? What could it be for?"

Doctor Sing began, "General Matthews, this is Marriam Daily and Sanjay Patel. They are two of my most trusted and talented researchers. They will be the only people allowed into this room while we attempt to establish what we have here. I will instruct them on how to set up this room for our research and how we will proceed. I will be the only other person allowed into this room, except for you, of course."

"Doctor, I'm sure you understand how sensitive this is. I don't want any information to leave this room while we record and monitor this. I don't want any conversations accidentally overheard and I especially don't want one word of this talked about or texted about on any cellphones."

Doctor Sing glanced over at his researchers who nodded.

Matthews continued, "All communications from this moment forward will be face-to-face."

"Understood, General."

"It's all yours, Doctor," Matthews said, placing the bag on the floor in the corner.

General Matthews walked from the room.

Doctor Sing turned his attention to Sanjay and Marriam and explained how he wanted the room to be set up. Afterward, he left them to complete their task.

Lab 126a

3:00 PM PDT

By 3:00, Marriam and Sanjay had completed Doctor Sing's instructions for the setup in the private room. There was one stable table with an adjustable device for holding something in place, a simple desk lamp similar to the one in General Matthews' office, three small tables that students used in classrooms, and three, fold-up chairs. There were also three small laptop computers and two digital cameras with night vision, atop tripods.

Once finished, Sanjay and Marriam sat staring at each other waiting for Dr. Sing's return and wondering what was in the bag. They had been instructed not to look inside.

Marriam was fidgety. She wore wire-rimmed glasses, had brown eyes and light brown hair pulled back into a ponytail. A bit pale and thin, she loved her work. She sat nervously biting a fingernail, wanting to get started.

Sanjay paced with his mind in overdrive trying to guess what was in the bag. He was young for a researcher, just twenty-five, but he had graduated at the head of his class at Stanford. While making far less than he could make in the private sector, he had a natural love for the work done at the infamous Area 51 and he had hoped to someday come face-to-face with something alien. It was a dream that money couldn't buy.

Doctor Sing walked back into the room carrying a computer server with nearly unlimited storage. He smiled a bit grimly as he stepped further into the room.

He said, "Sit down, Sanjay."

Sanjay sat by Marriam.

The Doctor sat facing them and began, "Now, we have a task. The reason that I wanted you both to be part of this is because you both have shown exceptional insight in your research. I'm going to show you something. It's what you'll be tasked to study for the foreseeable future."

Neither Marriam or Sanjay spoke.

Doctor Sing walked into the corner and lifted the gym bag, then carried it to the table, setting it on top.

Marriam and Sanjay watched.

Sing unzipped the bag and removed a blanket-wrapped object. He unwrapped it and stood back.

Sanjay said, "That's the fake thing that's been on the news."

"Yes," Doctor Sing responded.

"Then why are we looking at something fake?"

"Because we don't think it's fake."

Marriam stood and stepped towards the egg. "You mean that this is a real alien artifact?"

"That is what we think."

"Oh, shit," Sanjay said.

"Yep," Sing said placing the egg into its holder on top of the table and by the desk lamp. He then carried over the standup lamp. Next, he placed one of the cameras into a corner of the room and turned it on while connecting it to the computer server that he had brought in.

"This camera is to remain on, at all times, 24/7. No exceptions. It will record everything that happens in this room from this day forward."

Sanjay glanced at several cameras built into the room. "Why not just use the cameras in the room?"

"Because we're afraid that they could be hacked. Nothing digital will leave this room and I mean never. Nothing digital, except for what's here, will be allowed in. No cell phones, no laptops, no flash drives, and no pads. Nothing from the outside. Understand?"

They both nodded.

"I don't need to tell you how secret this is. I'm going to reiterate that you don't speak to anyone about this. You will enter using the back door into this place. Everyone else who works in this lab will be told that you've been reassigned to another lab and we will provide a suitable and boring reassignment alibi for you both."

"Okay?" Sanjay said a bit questioningly.

The Doctor looked at Sanjay grimly. "I don't think you're fully understanding the nature of your task. People will kill and torture you for this information. If anyone has any idea that you're working on this, you'll become a target. If I'm right about what this is and what it means, the United States of America is about to jump several million years ahead of everyone else on Earth and that means that America might also become a near-term target for our enemies because they will know that very soon we will have an overwhelming advantage over them. You've both seen or read the "Lord of the Rings," right?"

They both nodded.

"Well, this is all the rings and the one that rules them all."

Marriam went quite white. Sanjay sat with his mouth slightly open.

"Now, I think you're beginning to understand."

Marriam said, "And you're trusting us with this?" She looked askance.

"I will be the point person for this. You will report anything to me and I mean anything, any thought, any feeling, and intuition, no matter how small or insignificant you think it might be. It might be the key to the whole puzzle."

Marriam was not feeling any better about her new assignment. "What if someone finds out that we're working on this project?"

"Honestly, we think we have this pretty buttoned up. There was a bit of press on it originally, but it's beginning to die down. The government has convinced the guy who found it that the whole thing was a well-played hoax and to my knowledge, there are only six other people, not including you two, who know that we are taking this egg-thing seriously and one of the six is the President and the other is his Chief of Staff. The Vice-President doesn't even know."

Sanjay said, "So, what do we do now?"

"Go and clear out your desks. Tell everyone that you're being reassigned and you're pissed about it. Tomorrow you'll enter through the back-door, parking in that lot. No one you work with is allowed to park there and it's private, then you'll come in here and I'll show you what we know, so far. You will start at 6:00 AM, two hours before anyone else and you'll get off at 2:30, before everyone else goes home. You will pack your lunches. You will not be allowed to eat in the cafeteria. There is a bathroom just down the hall."

"I'm stressed," Marriam said honestly.

"I know, Marriam. Your country needs you. This is going to be bigger than the Manhattan Project. Now go and I'll see you in the morning. I have a lot to think about. I'm a bit stressed, myself."

"Doctor?" Sanjay said questioningly. "Why are you using us? Why don't you have some big team of specialists working on this thing? I don't understand."

"A couple of reasons. One is that we're not sure who to trust. Believe it or not, I trust you both more than people that I don't know. Marriam and I have worked together for more than five years and I know that I've only worked with you for a year, Sanjay, but I trust you also. Someone in the Manhattan Project, back in the 1940s, leaked most of the secrets learned there to the Russians. As I understand it, we are going to share this information with the entire world just as soon as we have discovered as much as we can. It would be far too destabilizing for our world not to do so, but we want to have all the information first, then we'll just have to let it out and hopefully trust the world to make the right decisions as to what to do with the information. We think that if aliens purposely left this for us to find, it has something to do with space travel. We don't know how much, but that's our current best guess."

Sanjay and Marriam rose and left the room leaving Doctor Sing running one hand through his hair and obviously tense. He glanced at the deflated, green gym bag sitting lonely in the corner, then the egg-thing in its new place on the desk and he breathed out deeply.

Chapter 8

Edwards Air Force Base

Lab 126a

August 15, 2085

5:50 AM PST

Sanjay followed Marriam as they both drove into the secure parking lot at 5:50 am. The sun had just begun to peek over the hills and throw its light onto the infamous Area 51 and the morning was warm and the air dry.

They both parked and emerged from their cars warily, then walked towards each other, half smiled, didn't speak and approached the back door to the lab. Two uniformed guards awaited them, watching as they neared.

As Marriam and Sanjay walked to the lab door, they each flashed their badges to the guards and expected the guards to open the secure door but the guards just stood back after checking their badges. There was a hand pad and Marriam shrugged and placed her left hand on the pad. The door didn't respond. Sanjay placed his hand on the pad and stood back a step. The door then slowly slid open.

Marriam glanced at the guards questioningly but they kept their mouths shut and their eyes forward. Sanjay and Marriam entered.

Doctor Sing was waiting just inside the door.

"Good morning," he said.

They both nodded.

Marriam said questioningly, "The hand pad didn't open the door for me? It only opened it for Sanjay."

"No, it recognized that there were two of you there and wouldn't open until you were both checked in. It also uses facial recognition and was able to identify you and the guards by that. There is tighter security here than where you worked before."

"Oh," she said.

The Doctor stepped down a short hallway followed by the researchers and continued, "You each have a locker in that room," he said pointing. "Your cell phones don't continue past this point."

Marriam and Sanjay stepped into the room and each locked their personal belongings. This had been standard procedure since they began as researchers.

Once finished, they continued to the lab, entering a second door with a retina scan, then onto the small room set up with the egg.

As they entered, the Doctor said, "Okay, here we go. Sit down and I'll bring you up to speed."

He walked over and turned on the desk lamp and moved it to shine directly on the metallic egg. He then went and sat down by Marriam and Sanjay. The Doctor was silent. Two minutes passed and then three. Nothing happened, but by the fourth minute, faint flashes of light began to show just under the clearcoat of the egg's exterior. Splashes of color in the form of fireworks burst and twinkled under what looked like a clear glass surface, which had looked solid metal just moments before.

Sanjay and Marriam sat silently as the egg went through what appeared to be its warmup. The aurora began then and squirmed over the surface of the egg, bathing it in green, blue and white. Once finished with the aurora, the egg began to glow a faint green, then a white light leaked from its surface. The hologram burst forth where the white light had appeared, showing blue and green columns of light leaping to around four feet above the egg's surface. Then the vertical lines and backslashes began to stream through the green columns of light connecting to other green columns in differing grids. The same then began with the blue columns.

Doctor Sing walked over and turned off the desk lamp and the egg seemed to power down with the hologram dimming, then going out altogether.

Doctor Sing asked, "Well, what do you think?"

Marriam was speechless.

Sanjay shook his head, then said questioningly, "Code of some kind?"

"That's what we think."

"Has anyone seen this egg-thing run longer?" Marriam asked. "I mean does the display change or do the columns just repeat themselves?"

"No one has seen it work much longer and the columns are too complexed to know that without study. That's where you come in. We think it's like a binary code with on and off switches but we don't know what the language is. We plan to video it, then run the slashes through a computer, but without knowing their language or them knowing ours, we don't think we'll be able to know exactly what it means. You see where we are right now?"

Sanjay and Marriam nodded solemnly.

"Time for you to get started," Doctor Sing stated. He got up and left the room.

They both sat unmoving for a minute, the wheels turning in their minds.

"Might as well turn it on," Marriam said.

Sanjay nodded and walked to the table holding the egg and turned on the desk lamp. He began filming with the second camera by switching it on and pointing it at the egg. This time the egg started a bit quicker as if it had stored a bit of the light's energy.

Everything happened as before, the fireworks, the aurora, and the columns of light. Both Sanjay and Marriam sat silently and watched.

"What now?" Sanjay asked, feeling a bit overwhelmed.

"Let's stop it and run the film through the computer, then start it again and see if it begins at the exact same spot."

"Sounds good."

By the end of the day, they thought that the egg was counting the times that it had been started and restarted because just two columns of the lines changed and those columns were the first that began each time. It appeared that one of the vertical lines would become a slash, each time the egg restarted. Then once the egg had started ten times a vertical line would become a slash in an adjacent column. Base ten?

By the end of the first week, it appeared that the egg was keeping tabs on how many times it was started using base ten, but none of the other columns that appeared changed in any way. When images of the columns were run through the computer, nothing of any substance was discovered.

By the end of the first month, nothing new had been learned. Marriam restarted the egg again and Sanjay, in complete frustration and staring at the egg from about a foot away, said loudly, "Marriam, we aren't going to learn anything. They should get someone else."

The egg started and just after the beginning sequence of vertical lines and slashes, a picture of Marriam showed in the hologram.

Sanjay's mouth fell open. "Shit," he whispered.

The picture winked out.

Marriam stood stark still, then walked towards the egg and stood by Sanjay. She brought her hand to her chest and said, "Marriam."

Her picture appeared again in the hologram. It winked out and the vertical lines and slashes returned.

She put her hand on Sanjay's shoulder and said, "Sanjay."

His picture appeared.

It winked out.

"Shit!" Sanjay said again, this time loudly.

His picture appeared again.

They both exploded into laughter.

"The egg thinks your name is Sanjay Shit!" Marriam said unable to contain herself.

"Damn. I'm going to have to stop using that word. You know what this means, don't you?!" Sanjay said excitedly.

"Yep. AI. It's some kind of artificially intelligent machine. It's learning... Damn."

Sanjay added, "We need to tell Doctor Sing, but more importantly, we need to figure out how to teach it."

Marriam was excited, but then she paused. "So, what if we teach it about us? What does that make it, a super-smart toy? I mean, how do we benefit from this as a country. Do you know what I mean?"

"I don't know, Marriam," Sanjay said, pausing and speaking at the machine.

The picture of Marriam appeared back in the hologram.

Marriam looked back at the egg. She said loudly,

"Doctor Sing."

His picture appeared.

Then she said, "General Matthews."

His picture appeared.

"Sanjay, do you remember the name of the guy who found this thing with the dinosaurs?"

"Ummm, I want to say, Wilson, I think that's it, Professor Wilson."

Marriam said, "Professor Wilson," directly at the egg.

The picture of a man in his sixties came up. They didn't know the professor but thought that it may be him.

Sanjay said, "It's been learning ever since it was exposed to light that first time. I wonder how much it knows?"

Marriam said, "Don't know, but let's talk to Doctor Sing and see what he says."

September 17, 2085

After Doctor Sing was apprised of Sanjay and Marriam's discovery that the 'egg' was learning, he discussed with several child and infant development experts about how babies learn. He then devised a system of pictures, movies, and linguistics in order to teach the machine the basics of human nature, society, speech, and communication.

October 24, 2085

By the end of the second month, the machine displayed some knowledge absorption but had not shown the ability to communicate.

Sanjay and Marriam stayed on the job as teachers for the machine exposing it to as much as possible and constantly reviewing the alphabet and numbers as we use them.

December 28, 2085

The third month began similarly to the second. The egg was now being shown computer language, first binary, then hexadecimal and C++. On Friday of the last week in that month, Marriam and Sanjay arrived at work in the morning. They chatted a bit, then turned the desk lamp onto the egg. The familiar flashes of fireworks began, then the aurora and last the columns of light. They sat and watched as the egg powered up. They had affectionately named the alien egg, 'Egbert.'

"What are we going to teach Egbert today?" Sanjay asked.

"Hmmm," Marriam said pouring over her notes and several communications from Doctor Sing.

Sanjay looked at the egg. His mouth fell open. Something had changed. Where before, there were columns of backslashes and vertical lines, now there were ones and zeros.

Marriam was staring at her notes and said, "Let's try…"

But she never finished the sentence. Sanjay silently put his hand on her head and turned her to look at Egbert.

Her mouth fell open. She said, "Ones and zeros!"

"Binary!" Sanjay said. "It's converted its code to our binary."

"Is the camera running?"

"Yep."

"Call Doctor Sing."

"I'm on it," Sanjay said jumping up and heading to the phone.

"Yes," Doctor Sing answered.

"You need to come down here, now," Sanjay said excitedly.

"I'm on my way."

They turned off the egg and sat, waiting for Doctor Sing to arrive.

He walked into the small room which hadn't changed from the first day.

"What's up?" he asked.

Marriam turned on the desk lamp.

"Just watch," Sanjay said.

The three sat down in the chairs and waited as the egg powered up.

Once the columns appeared, ones and zeros began to stream in the hologram. Doctor Sing watched with rapt attention.

"I think we did it. I think we broke the code," Sanjay said with some reverence.

Marriam said with the same reverence, "I think Egbert is about to give us his secrets."

"Egbert?" Doctor Sing said questioningly.

The ones and zeros stopped. In the hologram, a picture of the alien egg showed in the array.

The three laughed.

The picture of the egg faded and the ones and zeros proceded again to stream forward in the grids, just as the vertical lines and backslashes had before.

"Damn," Sing exclaimed. "What do you think it's trying to tell us?"

"I don't know," Marriam said, "But I can't wait to find out."

"Okay," the Doctor said. "Turn off the lamp and let's run these columns through the computer and see if we can get some idea of what they mean."

In the course of the day, the egg had run for a total of about fifteen minutes continuously. They isolated each column of ones and zeros and ran each through the computer. Three headings were displayed in plain English, that were represented by the columns of ones and zeros. The first was space flight, the second was terraforming a planet and the third was biological life extension. The columns that seemed to link with the ones and zeros connecting to the others, were thought to contain overlapping technology that must be applied to each. The world was about to change forever if this was a how-to manual for those three headings.

Doctor Sing said, "I need to get in touch with Matthews. I'm sure he will want to call the President."

Part 2

Space

Chapter 9

Las Vegas, Nevada

September 14, 2086

One year later...

Kirk Matthews Jr. sat in a bar stewing, leaning over a Jack Daniels, staring into its amber liquid and watching it caress the melting ice cubes. The fumes should be more soothing but they weren't. His father, Senator "Honest Kirk" Matthews, of Florida, had been calling all morning trying to get his son, Kirk Jr. back into college after he flunked out for the third time.

The Las Vegas bar was quiet and dark and seemed to be designed for those who had just lost their life savings and were on their way back home.

The cell phone rang, again, and Kirk, now on his second Jack Daniels, gazed at the phone blankly, then put it back in his pocket. It was noon and he drained the glass then asked the bartender for another. The bartender brought the drink and Kirk brought back out his phone and held it out to pay.

The bartender checked his transaction screen and said, "Thanks for the tip." He walked away to help someone else.

Kirk gazed into his new drink then softly said to himself, "I'm not going back to that school."

A woman passing by Kirk's barstool said, "What?"

He turned and looked over his shoulder not realizing that she was there. "Oh, no, I was talking to myself."

"That's not healthy but I guess we all do it."

"I guess."

The woman was probably in her early thirties with light brown hair cut short over her ears and feathery bangs. She was tall, thin and attractive with the look of a runner, wearing a short black skirt and was walking with two other ladies who were close to her age. The three women appeared to have been gambling.

Her two friends walked ahead to get a table but the woman lingered. She asked, "Having a bad day?"

Kirk half-smiled, "More like a bad year but it's mostly my own fault."

The woman turned to him. "It usually is but that doesn't make it any easier to take."

"Yeah."

She turned to her friends, who were motioning for her to join them. She said, "Got to go."

Kirk nodded.

She walked off and he glanced at her as she departed. She glanced over her shoulder at him, then joined her friends.

Kirk went back to his drink, slowly sipping and half-watching a football game on a small screen on the ceiling on one corner of the bar. The sound was off and closed-captioned words traveled along its bottom. A Keno screen flashed numbers from the casino, 18, 20, 66, 49.

He glanced over to where the three women were sitting. Two of them were talking animatedly but the woman who had talked to him earlier was looking his way. She made eye contact, looked away but then looked back at him. Her expression was... interesting.

Kirk turned back to stare at his drink. For it being his third, he should have felt it more but even the alcohol wasn't working. He kept his eyes down, hunched over his drink, and pondered his life in detail.

"Mind if I join you for a bit?" A female voice said from behind him. It was the woman who had talked to him earlier.

"No, sit down," Kirk said, looking over his shoulder and nodding at the empty chair beside him. He asked, "Where are your friends?"

"They deserted me. They wanted to go back and play the slots. Gambling just bores me."

"What are you drinking?" Kirk asked, motioning for the bartender.

"Vodka and cranberry."

The bartender asked, "What can I get you?"

"Get the lady a vodka-cranberry," Kirk said.

"With lime," she added.

"And I'll have another," Kirk said pointing at his Jack Daniels which was still half-full.

The woman said, "So, do you gamble?"

"No, I just come here to drink." Kirk raised his glass slightly and took a depressed sip.

The woman half-smiled and looked away.

Kirk emptied his glass.

The bartender came back with the new drinks and Kirk paid.

When the bartender walked away the woman asked, "What's your name?"

"Kirk."

"I'm Taylor. So, Kirk, why so glum?"

Kirk half-smiled and glanced glassy-eyed at Taylor then back at his drink. "I'm fucking up my life and can't seem to stop."

She nodded, sipping her drink. "Sounds serious."

"Oh... it is." He lifted his drink to his lips and downed half.

"By whose standards?"

"My father's, of course."

"Hmmm. You look a bit too old to define your whole life by your father's standards."

"Ya think?"

"Really, Kirk, what do you want from your life? I mean what would a successful life look like to you? Maybe you share your father's standards?"

"Well, I guess that's partially part of my problem. My father is extremely successful and I'm probably destined to work picking up litter in the park."

She shrugged, "I think a lot of those guys are pretty happy doing that."

"Yeah, I think you're right, but it wasn't what I figured for my life... What do you do?"

"I work at JPL in California. I monitor NEO's for a living."

Kirk perked up a bit. "Really, near-Earth objects. Now that's interesting."

"You know what NEO's are?"

"I do. You must enjoy your work."

"Yeah, I like it, but sometimes it's kind of spooky. I see things that could potentially end the world. I think if one of those asteroids were to hit us, I'd rather not see it coming."

Kirk smiled.

Taylor asked, "What does your father do that makes him so successful?"

Kirk breathed out, "Have you heard of Senator Kirk Matthews from Florida?"

"Sure, 'Honest Kirk.' He's one of NASA's biggest supporters. I've heard that he's saved the funding for the project that I work on, which, by the way, has also saved my job."

"That's him. I think he figured me for an astronaut, someday, not a royal screw-up."

Taylor shook her head. "I'm not going to feel sorry for you."

"Damn, I was hoping you would."

"Nope, sorry. No pity."

"My father's brother is General Matthews whose connected with Edwards Air Force Base."

"Oh, that's interesting. I've heard of your uncle, also. With two guys like that staring at you from their perch, it's no wonder you've lived under some pressure. I hear your father is thinking about a run for the Whitehouse."

"He's talked about it."

"He looks the part of a president, distinguished, has all his hair, not to mention that he's pretty handsome."

"I'm here to escape my father, not talk about how appealing he is."

"Oh, well, I find you pretty appealing, too, in a young, unsuccessful, pitiful kind of way, of course."

Taylor reached down and gently squeezed Kirk's thigh. "You have nice eyes," she said then added, "They're the most unusual color blue, almost violet."

Kirk asked, "Are you staying at this hotel?"

"Yep," she responded with a suggestive smile...

Arms, legs, sheets, breasts, pillows, gasping, then lips, a cascade of sights, smells, sounds, and sensation swirled around Kirk's muddled head. The alcohol had finally reached his brain and this woman, Taylor, was lean, passionate and willing, and was forcing his thoughts away from his problems.

They had been tangled in the sheets for nearly an hour when she arched and softly groaned with pleasure but continued to move with him. He kissed a breast. It was his turn then and he reached, then they slowed.

She found his lips again and kissed him gently but not the way she had kissed him before. He rolled off of her and they laid embraced for some moments, pushing the sheets down and off of their sweating bodies to cool.

They separated.

Taylor pushed her sweat-dampened hair off of her face with both hands and they rested, looking at the ceiling for a couple of minutes, not talking.

Taylor breathed out, turned to look at the clock, sat up, draped her legs over the side of the bed, then glanced over her shoulder at Kirk.

He turned to her and looked at her bare back, lean and athletic. She smiled at him a bit grimly then stood and rummaged around the floor for her panties which had come off in a flurry of passion. She found them under the nightstand and turned to face Kirk, saying. "You got to go." She pulled them on.

Kirk looked at her not quite understanding. "Might I see you again?"

"Nope. I'm flying out tonight to go back home."

"But…"

"Kirk, I'm married, though probably not for much longer. I'm not looking for complications." She looked around for her bra. She continued, "I'm sorry but I think I needed you as much as you needed me, today. My life is a bit on the screwed-up side, also."

She found the bra between a chair and a table by the window and reached down, picking it up, then paused contemplatively holding it in both hands. She glanced down onto the bustling strip some twelve floors below, then turned back to Kirk and said a bit dreamily, "You know, this was pretty empty." She found Kirk's eyes then finished, "Sex should be a celebration." She fastened the bra behind her and turned away.

Kirk nodded and rose silently, now feeling quite naked and a bit used and he dressed. Once finished, he looked over at Taylor who was buttoning her shirt. He asked, "Any final words of wisdom for me?"

"Yep. Get your head out of your ass, Matthews. You don't want the only thing that people say about you is that you have nice eyes and you're a good lay."

He nodded and grinned a bit sheepishly, then walked from the room. As the door closed, he pulled out his phone. Six missed calls.

He breathed out, walked to the elevator, pushed the down button and waited. He thought about Taylor. He liked her, but she had her own demons right now. He figured that he would never see her again… Too bad… The elevator door opened and his phone rang. He didn't look at it as he stepped in, then he turned and faced the elevator doors which slid closed in front of him.

Chapter 10

Edwards Air Force base

October 1, 2086

11:00 AM PST

General Jeffery Matthews sat behind his desk, contemplating how to proceed. The alien egg, 'Egbert,' as it had become affectionately known, had, as close as they could tell, revealed most of its secrets. The most intriguing aspect of it was its A.I. which could answer limited questions about the information contained inside of its shell. The General had been forced to allow the knowledge of it to extend to a few others outside the original inner circle, including several members of Congress, which happened to include his brother, Senator 'Honest Kirk' Matthews.

Initially, Doctor Sing, and his two assistants, Marriam Daily, and Sanjay Patel, had been the only people on Earth besides himself, President Dent and his Chief of Staff to know, for sure, that the alien egg was being studied. Portis, the head of security, knew of its existence and where it was being kept but didn't know the extent of the study or if anything was being discovered.

The problem was that reoccurring rumors abound about the alien egg and what it was. No sooner would the State Department quash one rumor, then another would arise. It would show up on the internet and would have its own life as it made its way around most of the social media sites. Then it would die down for a bit only to arise again.

The General had needed to make several decisions on his own about how to proceed with the information that the egg had revealed. Some were easy, some not so much. The egg had, in no uncertain terms, warned of the destructive powers of asteroids and comets. It stressed the need to build several asteroid killing space stations that could be placed between the Earth and the potential hazard of a collision. Though space was an exceedingly dangerous place anyway, the most pressing and solvable issue for the survivability of the human race was an extinction event by an asteroid. Someone or something had deposited the egg on Earth, and for some reason, wanted humans to survive.

Matthews sat back in his chair contemplating the alien egg. It had revealed a huge amount of information and was spectacular in designing space stations by modifying its own designs to use current human technology. The alien egg also needed to know about human biology and all the studies of how space affected us. It worked into the station's designs, a gravity producing force that mimicked the approximate gravity of Earth and shielding against the destructive DNA shredding particles from the sun, which used antimatter contained in a space station induced magnetic field, some of which was then used for fuel.

Considering all of this, 'Egbert' had little other information that didn't concern its three main objectives.

Human life would need to be extended to move into space, the Earth would need to be protected from asteroid strikes, humans would need other planets in which to inhabit and the alien egg would need to provide the necessary technology to achieve these goals.

When asked questions outside of the egg's specified goals, like to explain the Grand Unification Theory, which Einstein spent the end of his life trying desperately to uncover, and no one else since, had been any more successful in finding, the egg would simply say that it didn't contain that information. When asked where 'Egbert' was from, or who placed the alien egg on Earth, it repeated the same response, it didn't contain that information. Sanjay asked it about God but its response was the same, it did not contain that information. Sanjay asked it to speculate but its response was the same.

Marriam and Sanjay began to discuss the fact that some scientists, out there, might want to cut 'Egbert' open and thereby ruining it, so Marriam asked the egg for detailed blueprints of how it was designed. The response was the same, it did not contain that information.

It seemed to be designed to get us into space and to help us survive as a species but nothing more.

General Matthews had begun the design and manufacturing of the components needed to assemble the first asteroid killing space station and the terraforming devices. Everything learned from this would move the United States a hundred years or more above the rest of the world technologically but could be achieved with little-unwarranted attention, at least, at first, since most of the design was current technology that was already in use. If handled correctly, it would seem like nothing more than normal U.S. policies.

The more controversial plan was to terraform Mars. Matthews struggled with this decision. Was that something that they should attempt? Was it moral? Might they be destroying or disrupting something important by attempting to terraform Mars and make it more earthlike? He left the final decision for that to the President who told him to proceed but quietly.

The egg had identified the red planet as the best candidate in which to proceed with terraforming. That was a no-brainer. It had significant water in the form of ice at its poles and newly discovered ice, just under most of its surface. If more water was needed, the alien egg had a plan to steer comets to collide with Mars which would deposit more water as needed and thicken the atmosphere. The next planet to be terraformed would be Venus. The alien egg stated that the terraforming of Venus would take hundreds of years but that it could be done. It was within the safe region of space for human habitation.

The problem with terraforming any planet was that something like that should take millions of years at best but with the technology provided by Egbert, the process for Mars would be well on its way in ten Earth years. The process would include thickening the atmosphere, increasing the magnetic field and the ozone layer, the melting of available ice for usable water, and the adjusting of the planet's atmospheric pressure, then the seeding of Earth-born bacteria, plants and eventually, animals. Melting the carbon dioxide-rich ice caps alone would fill the atmosphere with greenhouse gasses, thickening it and beginning the process of heating the planet. There was a reasonably established theory that Mars had, at one time, been like Earth until something happened to strip off most of the atmosphere leaving it barren, but with a nudge, it could possibly be inhabitable by humans in the not too distant future. The new atmosphere might not last forever but most scientists thought that a new atmosphere could last for several millions of years, long enough.

The components for the first prototype of the devices used to begin the terraforming of Mars were just beginning to be manufactured as small, insignificant components for an unknown device. General Matthews used several different manufacturers to produce these components, all trusted defense contractors and all based in the U.S. The device would be assembled at Edwards Airforce base in six months and then three separate devices would be launched to Mars, each containing their portion of the terraforming procedure to begin the processes. They would be launched under the guise of Martian probes. The terraforming would begin without the world knowing anything about it.

General Matthews was anxious, but he knew he had to proceed with caution and keep this project as small as possible for as long as possible. The construction of the critical portions of the terraforming machines would need to be kept more than top secret.

Edwards Air Force Base

General Matthews Office

October 29, 2086

General Matthews sat at his desk when a call came in from Doctor Sing.

He said, "General, we need to see you."

"I'll be right there."

Matthews left his office and drove to the lab where 'Egbert' was being kept. He arrived at the back door, went through security and walked into the lab.

Doctor Sing, Sanjay Patel, and Marriam Daily waited outside of the alien egg's containment room. They all stood with grim expressions.

Matthews walked up.

"General," Doctor Sing started. "The egg has revealed something that you need to see."

"Okay," Matthews said.

"This came up in its display without us asking for it. The egg volunteered the information."

"Okay?"

The desk light had been left on, powering the egg and a hologram floated above its exterior. In the hologram, there appeared to be a starfield and in it, as the main focal point was a sun and orbiting planets that were not moving. It was obviously our system fixed in time.

"This looks like us, am I right?"

"Yes," Doctor Sing responded. "Watch. There's the third planet, us."

"Egbert, show us 2101."

The solar system began moving at what appeared to be a normal rate, then sped up with the planets revolving quickly around the sun and the moons revolving quickly around each planet with the dates rolling in the upper left-hand corner of the hologram. You could see asteroids come and go, entering the solar system, then exiting in their own orbits. The display then slowed the planet's orbits around the sun and the dates and time slowed to 2101. January, February, March, April, 1st of May, 2nd of May, 3rd of May. 12:00 AM through to 6:25 AM and 20 seconds, then boom!

Earth was struck by a huge asteroid and the hologram went black.

"Damn," Matthews said. "Do we have a problem? Is this just an illustration to scare us, or are we in this asteroid's path?"

"We've run this several times and it's always the same, on the exact day and time, and then it goes black, like no more humans."

"Damn," Matthews whispered, again. "Doctor Sing, plot the trajectory of this asteroid. If we can identify it, maybe we can stop it."

"That was my hope," Doctor Sing said. "It won't be a problem to plot, but from the probable size of the asteroid and its incredible speed, stopping it is going to be like stopping a freight train with a Volkswagen Bug. This came from beyond the Ort cloud, not the asteroid belt just beyond Mars. To our knowledge, nothing in the asteroid belt is this large. Another thing, its orbit takes millions of years. I asked Egbert to plot its orbit and its last pass was before the dinosaurs."

"Huh?" Matthews said trying to get his head around that. He shook it and said, "That leaves us fifteen years. Get me the coordinates, I'm already working on the solution."

"Yes, Sir," Sing responded.

Chapter 11

Air Force Academy

Colorado Springs, Colorado

January 5, 2088

Two Years Later…

Shortly after Kirk Matthews Jr. had his *'roll in the hay'* with Taylor, and she suggested that he remove his head from where the sun don't shine, he had a meeting with his father the Senator. It was a frank discussion and his father, though disappointed at his son's failure in college, pulled some strings with the help of Uncle Jeffery, AKA, General Matthews, and got Kirk Jr. into the Air Force Academy. It helps to know influential people.

Kirk thought about Taylor, who he had met in Las Vegas and whose last name he hadn't acquired. She worked in California for JPL… And he wondered about her. There was something about her that wouldn't let her escape his memory… And in those quiet moments, when he was alone and his mind was adrift, her face would appear as if by magic.

At that time, Kirk had come to one of those moments in life where you're walking towards a cliff, and it's in full view, and you back away, or jump. He chose the wiser of the two.

He buckled down in school, staying near the top of his class with the help of his 120 I.Q. and was off to the next part of flight school. He wanted to fly the next generation of stealth fighter just off the design floor of Lockheed Martin. These were thought to be the last of the manned fighters and each would command six drones that would fly with it and would be commanded by the stealth pilot and co-pilot effectively increasing the Air Force, six-fold. Each drone could be let loose autonomously to protect the fighter or could be controlled by the pilot to attack various targets. The United States was about to take a considerable leap forward with this fighter for several reasons. First, it could fly higher and faster than any previous fighter made by any country, but it could also release its drones to intercept ICBMs launched at the United States. Each drone had a secret weapon not previously known to man. It could emit an intense, limited range, EMP (electromagnetic pulse) shockwave at a target frying its electronics which would send it crashing to Earth, or the drone could attach itself to a target, and once the electronics were disabled, take the target into space, though once in space, could not return.

Rogue nations like North Korea or Iran, which had been threatening different countries with their acquired nuclear weapons were going to be rendered ineffective by the use of this new fighter dubbed, The Dome Raptor because once fully deployed, would create an impenetrable dome over the United States.

***

It was three days before flight school was to begin and Kirk was excited. He called his two best friends from the program, Sandy Jones, and Jason Chapman and talked them into meeting him at a bar near the base. It was a common hangout for anyone working on the Air Force base or attending the academy.

The place was half-full of only men, playing pool and watching sports. The bar must have been there for a hundred years with its worn wooden floors and cedar paneling. A polished wooden bar counter ran its length and was lined with chairs where several men sat. The sound of dice cups thumping on the bar rang-out as the men rolled for drinks. Behind the bar was a smoky mirror atop a counter that was lined with bottles of liquor along its full length. An old fashion cash register set on one side of the bar for anyone who might still use cash, though not many did any longer. Most cash transactions just went into the owner's pocket without being rung-up.

Kirk sat at a table and was eating chips and guacamole. He had a tall beer in a frosted mug and watched several different sporting events on several different televisions that were suspended from the ceiling, from various places, around the bar.

Jones walked in. He was African American with friendly eyes and a million-dollar smile, not tall at five-eight but he stood straight and appeared to be taller than his measured height. His father had been military, Navy, and it seemed the children of former military just naturally moved and acted as if born to it. He saw Kirk at his table and he smiled as he walked over.

Kirk waved at the bartender for another beer and the bartender poured it from the tap and set it on the bar.

"Hey, Jonesy," Kirk said to Sandy.

Jones sat down. Kirk jumped up and got Sandy the beer.

"Thanks," Jones said.

Kirk asked, "Seen Chapman yet?"

"No, I haven't seen him at all, today."

"He said he'd be here."

Kirk pushed the chips at Jones. "Help yourself."

"Thanks."

"Are you ready for flight school?"

"I think so," Jones said crunching a chip. "You ready?"

"Yeah, but I think it's about to get real out there," Kirk said.

"Yep, no one fires simulated missiles at you in the real world."

Kirk said, "I'm glad you're going there with me, and Chapman, too. To be honest, I'm kind of spooked."

Chapman walked in. He was taller than both Jones and Matthews at nearly six-three, thin with a pale complexion and a continually serious expression. He rarely seemed to smile, though he was generally a pretty happy guy.

He saw Jones and Matthews and walked up to the table. He said, "Sorry, I'm late. I was talking to my sister."

"Oh, is she cute?" Kirk asked.

"I don't know! And who looks at their sister that way! Besides, she wouldn't be right for your sorry ass, anyway."

"Geeze," Kirk said. "Why so defensive?"

"She's going through a tough time right now. She's in the middle of a bad divorce. The guy's being a jackass."

"Oh?" Kirk said. "Me and Sandy were just drinking to flight school."

"And eating guacamole," Sandy said. "I love this stuff."

"I'll get you a beer, Chapman. Sit down," Kirk said.

Obviously depressed, Chapman said, "Make it two."

Chapman grabbed a chip and aggressively dunked it.

Kirk jumped up and as he was walking back to the table carrying the two beers, both for Chapman, he glanced at the door and his mouth fell open. There, stepping in was Uncle, General Jeffery Matthews, flanked by a captain and a major. All were in full uniform. Everyone military stood.

"As you were," The General said.

Kirk walked to the table and set down the drinks.

General Matthews saw Kirk and walked to greet him.

General Matthews said, "Hello, Kirk. I was looking for you. Got a minute?"

Jones and Chapman hadn't sat back down and they surreptitiously glanced at Kirk.

"Hi, General. Sure, want a beer?"

"No. I need to talk to you in private for a minute."

"Okay? Is everything okay?"

"Oh, yeah."

"Okay? Where do you want to talk?"

"Step outside with me?"

Kirk glanced at his two shocked friends, then said to the General, "Sure," and to his friends, "I'll be back in a minute."

Kirk followed General Matthews and the two other officers outside the bar. They stopped a few feet from the door.

Kirk said, "How'd you know I was here?"

"I had you followed," General Matthews said with a wry grin.

"Oh. Seems like a lot of trouble."

"I actually wanted to catch you at the school before I had to leave, but I was tied up and couldn't get away, so I told my Staff Sargent to follow you. I wanted to talk to you in person."

Kirk nodded.

"Kirk, this is Captain Freeman and Major Padilla."

"Sirs," Kirk said shaking their hands.

General Matthews began, "You did very well in school and now you're about to start flight school?"

"That's right."

"Kirk, I have another idea that I would like you to consider."

"Really, well, as long as it isn't Special Forces. I don't think I could deal with that much discomfort."

The General smiled and said, "No, that's for a special kind of soldier. This is something else."

"Okay. Would this include flight school?"

"In a way, but a different kind. I can't discuss it fully here but we are going into space and I mean full blast, and we're pulling around forty guys like you from the different military flight schools as a start and giving them a different kind of training. Come and see me tomorrow in my office and I'll outline it fully, say 0900 hours. I think you'd be perfect for the program and I'm sure your father would agree."

General Matthews handed Kirk a card. "This is the address of my office here in Colorado."

Kirk nodded. "I'll see you tomorrow."

"Oh, and, Kirk, don't discuss this with anyone, especially over the phone. That's why I'm connecting with you here, in person."

"Okay."

Kirk watched as the three officers stepped into a limousine and drove off...

Space, what could that mean, exactly? He knew how limited outer space was for humans with its vast distances, frigid temperatures, and destructive particles. It truly was no place for people, unless they were on a planet, of course.

He shook his head and walked back into the bar.

Jones and Chapman were finishing the last of the guacamole and chips. They both turned and watched as Kirk walked up.

Chapman said, "Okay, jackass, why didn't you tell us that you had a connection with General Matthews?"

"Yeah, Kirk," Jones said. "He seemed to be a lot more familiar with you than General to ass wipe."

"He's my uncle, and you'd better give me a bit more respect or I'll have him station both of you in Antarctica."

Jones said, "Seriously, Kirk, you should have told us."

"Look, I've had him and my father looking over my shoulder all of my life. I try to avoid thinking about them if I can help it."

Chapman said, "So, who's your father, The Pope?"

"Have you ever heard of Senator Kirk Matthews?"

"Yeah," Jones said.

Chapman said, "No, but I recognize the name. Oh, yeah, that's because it's your name, minus the 'Ass Wipe' in the middle of course."

"He's a big deal, too," Jones said.

Chapman said, "He is? So, what happened to you, Kirk, did someone drop you on your head as a baby?"

"Hey hey, where's the love?" Kirk laughed. "Here's a bit of my story. I was not excelling as a human, so they got me into the academy. I had to pass the tests of course, but I admit that I needed help finding a direction. They stepped up and gave me a hand, one that I didn't necessarily deserve."

"Ahhhh," Chapman said, not quite finished giving Kirk a bad time yet. "Spoiled brat."

"Yep, and now I need another beer and since you both ate all the guacamole, some more of that, too."

Kirk got up and came back with chips, guacamole and another beer for himself and one for Jones.

"So, why was the General so hot to talk to you in private?" Chapman asked with his mouth half-full of chip and dip.

"I'm not sure. He wants me to meet him at his office, tomorrow."

"He didn't say anything?" Jones asked.

"Yeah. He said something that I'm not supposed to repeat."

"Wooh," Chapman said.

"I think he wants me to do this other thing instead of flight school."

Jones said, "But you've worked so hard to get to flight school. Very few people actually make it."

"I guess I'll find out tomorrow."

Chapter 12

Air Force Academy

Colorado Springs, Colorado

January 6, 2088

0600 Hours MST

Kirk had risen early and put in three miles at a track on base that surrounded a practice football field. He was bundled up in grey sweats with a black Colorado Rockies baseball cap on backward. Frost clung on the track as the morning was cold with no breeze and the rising sun, which hadn't cleared the hills, colored the sky with orange and red.

Through the entire run, Kirk's mind was on his Uncle's visit to the bar yesterday... Space? What could the United States be doing in space that no one would know about? Most things accomplished in space these days were done by private companies. Even military satellites were put into orbit on rockets built by these companies. Most governments had stepped back from space because of the enormous costs.

Finished with his run, he jogged back to the dorm room that he shared with three other guys. Two of them still slept, while the third was gone. He grabbed a change of clothes and headed to the showers.

After breakfast, Kirk drove the short distance to his Uncle's office at the Academy…

General Matthews Office

Colorado Springs, Colorado

0900 Hours MST

Kirk Matthews walked into the waiting room of his Uncle's office. A receptionist sat typing and as he entered, she glanced up.

"Hello, I'm Kirk Matthews. I have a 9:00 appointment with the General."

"Hi, Mister Matthews. Have a seat and I'll tell him you're here."

Kirk sat straight in a chair. The waiting room reminded him of a doctor's waiting room without the magazines. The chair was padded, but stiff and he gazed out a window onto the grounds of the academy that he had called home for the past two years.

The receptionist said, "He'll see you now."

Kirk, with a somber expression, turned to her and nodded, stood, then walked into the General's office.

General Matthews was sitting behind a large desk in a comfortable chair staring at Kirk as he entered the room. Kirk was nervous. He had never been nervous around his uncle before. Until now, his uncle had always been Uncle Jeff. At family gatherings, he was funny and charming and it was obvious that Uncle Jeff loved Kirk's father, the Senator. They had always seemed close.

"Good morning, Kirk. Have a seat."

Kirk sat on one of two high-backed chairs that faced the General's desk. Kirk had never had any trouble talking to his uncle before, but now he felt tongue-tied.

"Let me get to it," the General said, sitting back in his chair with his hands folded in his lap. He was in full uniform, not including coat and hat. "We are going into space as a country, Kirk, and maybe as a world. I want to give you a chance to consider if this might be something that would appeal to you."

"I'm not sure. Space scares me. It's dangerous up there."

"So is flying fighter jets."

"Yeah, but you get to land back on Earth."

"By this time next year, we are going to launch several space stations manned by asteroid killing equipment. We have plotted several asteroids that may, within the next fifteen years, plow into our planet. These are big babies and while they might not kill all life on Earth, they would make it miserable. One, in particular, could finish us. We are going to take them out, permanently."

"How long would I be up there?"

General Matthews paused, leaning back in his seat. "Okay, so, I want to level with you. I wouldn't tell you this, but you are family and your father already has this information because I just told him recently. You might not ever come back to Earth. I'm not saying that this is a one-way trip, for sure, but we are going to embark on the next step for the human race. We are going to terraform and colonize Mars. We now have the technology to do so, and the first two terraforming machines have been launched and are on their way. It will begin a process that will take around ten years from the start until we think we can begin to introduce bacteria. The job of the first two machines will be to melt Mars' polar ice caps and will begin to increase the magnetic field around the planet. They will only start that process. Melting the polar ice caps will start the process of thickening the atmosphere. We have a third machine, but it's being delayed because of some technical difficulties. Even with all that, humans might still not be able to live on the planet. Gravity is going to be a problem, but we might be able to grow plants and some animals there. Before we can step foot on the planet, there will be large domed villages built partially into the ground."

"No offense, Uncle, General, Sir, but did you hit your head. I mean I love you, and you have always been nearly as close to me as my father, but this sounds like you've slipped a cog."

General Matthews smiled, "I'm going too, Kirk. I'm going to Mars in five years to oversee the building of the first domed cities. These cities will, at first, do the job of pushing the terraforming forward. There will be twenty cities built within two years of that time. These cities will be very small at first, no more than outposts, spread out evenly over the Martian surface, each will have terraforming machines specific to changing the Martian atmosphere to be more like Earth's which will include an ozone layer and an increased magnetic field. They will also be charged with seeding Mars with bacteria and plants to increase greenhouse gases to raise the temperature, not to mention, taking the readings and tracking how the terraforming is progressing. At some point, I want you to come to Mars to live in the first colonies. If this goes well, each of these outposts will be constantly expanded to accommodate the growing populations of people migrating from Earth and the children born native to the Martian planet. Think of it, native Martians. Sounds like something out of Jules Vern. We have also identified more than a few comets that we are going to steer into the planet. They are ice-filled and the collision will add water and help to thicken the atmosphere."

Kirk's eyes widened and he shook his head. "This is a lot to take in."

"I know. I need you to keep all this information to yourself. It's highly classified, for now. You can talk it over with your father, of course, he has been completely briefed, but it must be face to face. We can't take any chances that a cell phone transmission could be intercepted.

At first, you and the other new flight school pilots are going to be trained to fly asteroid killing vehicles. These vehicles will be equipped with weapons powerful enough to destroy or divert any asteroids bound for Earth or Mars. Within one hundred years, we plan to move out to the moons of the outer planets. Uranus, Neptune, Jupiter, and Saturn all have moons that are suitable for our purposes."

"And you plan to terraform them also?" Kirk asked, not hiding his skepticism.

"No, but we plan to build domed cities on the planet's moons. The ones with ice that can be converted to water."

"I feel like I want to say no," Kirk said, beginning to lose his uncertainty.

"Two weeks ago, we launched the first space station designed to move us further out into space. It will eventually be a fueling and docking port. It's further out than other space stations have been in the past and it will be located behind the Moon where it will remain for now, so no one on Earth can monitor it by telescope. It's still a work in progress and we will be adding to it in the months to come before it's fully functional, but it's already up there and on its way to the Moon. It will also oversee the first prototype of the small domed outposts scheduled to be built on Mars. It's going to be constructed on the dark side of the Moon. Again, it will be out of view from the rest of the world."

"That sounds like a lot of stuff to get up into space, not to mention some 230,000 miles to the Moon."

"I'm military, Kirk, logistics is what we do. You can't move any army without moving stuff. The space station has rendezvoused with several huge containers that had been sent to space two weeks before its launch. The space station will drag them, like a tugboat, to its destination on the dark side of the Moon. There, it will be assembled and completed."

"Huh."

"Kirk, we need people we can trust for this venture. There will be a time, up there, when you will be asked if you wish to stay or go home. If you choose to stay, you won't be able to come back home. I'm never coming back to Earth, Kirk. This is my destiny."

Kirk's eyes raised at that and his mind began to whirl but he said, "I don't know."

"In two months from now, the first group of trainees for what I would like you to do, are going up there to train. I would like you to go."

"In two months? Can't I just train here?"

"Most of the people selected will get their beginning training here but we are going to need trainers for them once they reach space. I was hoping that you might be one of those."

"But I've never flown anything?"

"Flying something in space isn't like flying something in Earth's atmosphere. There's no friction up there, nothing to slow you. It's not the same."

Kirk smiled at the thought. It wasn't conscious, it was subtle but it showed and the General saw it.

"Now you're getting it, Kirk. This is the biggest thing that's ever happened to humans. Take some time to think about it but not long. We're going to space."

Kirk's mind slipped from his musings and back to the situation. He asked, "What happened, Uncle? I don't get it. What caused this huge change? This is too much, too fast."

"Can't tell you that right now but humans are about to take a quantum leap forward."

"This feels rushed, which means that it feels dangerous."

"Oh, it's dangerous."

"Does the rest of the world know what the United States has planned for Mars?"

"Not yet," the General said with a flat expression.

Kirk considered his uncle's expression more than his words, then said, "I don't think that they're going to appreciate it."

"We've decided that, for the short term, they're not going to know."

"When would I go into training for this new assignment?"

"I would like you to start Monday. You have a lot to learn before you can go into space. You'd be getting a crash course."

"Here?"

"Nope, Edwards Air Force Base in California."

Kirk paused, "Is there anything else?" Kirk asked uncomfortably.

"No. You're excused. I need to know in the next couple of days."

Kirk nodded, didn't speak and walked from the room.

Chapter 13

As General Matthews watched Kirk walk from his office, the General sat and thought. The circle of people who knew about this project was growing exponentially. Keeping this entire project secret for much longer was going to be nearly impossible, but having all the components and parts to the space stations and terraforming machines purchased separately then assembled partially on Earth at Edwards, and partially in space should help it stay secret for a while but for how long? Another problem was the number of flights that were going to start leaving Earth. There was going to be an inordinate amount of activity that the world would surely notice. And they will know that we're heading to the Moon. Just short-term problems, he hoped, as the nations of Earth will eventually have to be part of this plan. It was just too enormous.

A call came into General Matthews from Edwards Air Force Base.

"Yes," Matthews answered.

"We have a problem with the space station."

"I'm on my way back."

General Matthews left his office, calling for his helicopter to be ready. In fifteen minutes, he was in the air.

Once back at Edwards Air Force Base, General Matthews was appraised of a problem with the space station's ability to collect antimatter trapped in the Earth's magnetic field. This was one of the alien egg's most amazing secrets. Antimatter is an atom in which the nucleus, which normally contains positively charged protons and neutrons, contains negatively charged particles. There are many problems with containing and using antimatter including storage because anytime an antimatter particle comes in contact with a positively charged particle, it is annihilated.

The alien egg had the solution for this by adjusting a magnetic field to trap the antimatter and funnel it into the space station's two ion engines as needed.

The antimatter would be contained in an artificially produced magnetic field that surrounded the space station, theoretically allowing the space station controlled, unlimited power. All of this design was from Egbert, of course, and none of it was thoroughly tested. The United States was in a big hurry and decided to trust Egbert. It was a huge leap of faith and one, so far, rewarded.

General Matthews took the problem to Doctor Sing, who ran it by the always eager 'Egbert.' Five minutes later, 'Egbert,' had the solution and once forwarded to the antimatter engineer on board the space station, the station was back on track with little more than a slight adjustment.

Two days later, the space station which had connected itself to four enormous containers was back on its way to the dark side of the Moon. Estimated time of arrival, four Earth days.

Chapter 14

Air Force Academy

Colorado Springs, Colorado

0600 Hours MST

A frigid wind blew through the pine trees with a ghostly moan, and the day's temperature dipped below zero. Kirk had just come back from a run breathing hard with plumes of heated breath being pushed from heaving lungs. He twisted at the decision that he would need to make. He considered flying to Florida to seek his father's advice on whether or not to go to space, but inside, he already knew. He would go. Despite all his fears, it was exactly what he wanted to do. In fact, it was what he had been waiting for, though he hadn't known it, for his entire life.

He jogged up the steps of his dorm and to his room where he grabbed a change of clothes and then headed to the showers.

His face was still ice cold from the run but steam filled the room with several men showering in the open locker room style showers. He quickly stripped and walked onto the tiled floor, turning on the shower, then extending his hand, and feeling for the water to get hot. When it did, he stepped in and let the water warm his body which had never really warmed up during his run. He should have dressed warmer. The cold seemed to go right through him. The water began to raise his body temperature and his mind drifted to his decision as he tried to consider the downside. All the, 'why he shouldn't,' easily outweighed the upside, but that didn't matter. He would go.

He finished and toweled off, dressed and as he was walking back to his dorm room, pulled his cell phone from his pocket.

He called General Matthews and after a short wait, as the receptionist rang the General, Kirk was put through.

"Hi, Kirk," General Matthews said.

"I'm in, Uncle. When do I go to Edwards?"

"Monday. Get packed."

"Yes, Sir."

"I'll see you here, Kirk."

"You're already there?"

"Yep. Had to deal with an issue. Talk to you later. Oh, and Kirk, keep this reassignment to yourself."

"Yes, Sir."

Kirk put his phone back in his pocket. He breathed out, feeling both afraid and exhilarated. His life was about to change. It sounded like, from what the General was saying, the world was about to change, also.

Chapter 15

Space Station Isla Alpha

The Dark Side of the Moon

January 12, 2088

1500 Hours PST

Space Station, Isla Alpha, had just arrived at its designated location at the Moon's equator on its dark side. The antimatter collection that had taken place in the Earth's Van Allen Belt had been successful and the station had, in its own artificially produced magnetic field, gathered enough to sustain the station and the building and operation of Moon Base Oasis for at least the next year. All of this technology was so new that no one was quite sure how long or how well it would work, but the trip to the Moon, some 230,000 plus miles, went smoothly. The space station also had normal human technology built in as a back-up in case Egbert's technology failed, but it would just be for an emergency and to buy enough time to try to rescue the crew.

Two of the large containers that the space station had been pulling would be deposited onto the Moon's surface and then a work crew would land and begin assembling the first domed outpost.

The space station itself was large. It carried twenty crew that were attached just to the space station alone, then another twenty-five men and women who would be used in different construction jobs. They would be transported to the Moon's surface to construct the domed outpost which consisted of three domes, each thirty feet in diameter and fifteen feet tall. Each would be connected to the other by hallways made of the same material. The initial construction would include life support, but not contain food or water, which would come later, and should take no more than a couple of weeks to complete.

Next, the construction crews would be tasked to complete the space station whose finished design would have it resemble a wagon wheel from the old west. On the center of the station, large engines would push it as it spun on an axle that contained a forward nose and the trailing antimatter engines. The wheel itself would have eight spokes which would attach to a central command in the middle with an outer ring that will contain sleeping, living and working quarters.

The wheel would then spin and once it reached optimum speed, would mimic the gravitational pull of Earth using centrifugal force. The outer ring will have gravity but as you move into the spokes and towards the center, the gravity will decrease until you reach the middle where the workers will be back in zero gravity. The plan was that eventually, all work that wasn't maintenance would move to the outer ring in order to limit the effects of zero-G on the body.

When the space station was launched, it was only the command module and two of the eight spokes, one pointing towards the station's destination and one pointing away, back to Earth. The ring and the other six spokes would need to be assembled in space, a daunting task.

The space station's Captain, Justin Chambers called the foreman for the building crew, Colonel Joseph Singleton, into his meeting room.

Singleton entered, floating through the door, tall and straight, in military greens. In his forties, he was career military and had been in several conflicts where his crews were charged with building temporary airbases for forward operations. Erecting things fast and tearing them down was his specialty, but he had never had to accomplish it in an environment like the Moon's dark side before. They had practiced in their spacesuits and underwater, but nothing could fully prepare them for a landscape as alien as the Moon's surface.

Chambers sat at the meeting table, with his seat belt on in zero gravity and the foreman floated to a seat across from the captain and strapped in.

The captain said, "Colonel Singleton, are your crews ready to proceed to the surface?"

The building crews just had a short window to complete their tasks. The dark side of the Moon is not continually dark. It has two weeks of darkness and two weeks of light when the sun shines on it. The reason that it's called the dark side of the Moon is a euphemism because it is "dark," to the view from Earth as we only see the side that faces us. The plan was for the crews to have finished the prefabbed outposts by the time the two weeks of daylight ended.

"Yes, Sir."

"The containers have been deposited there and await you. Take your crew to the shuttle bay. Oh, and Joseph, be careful down there. We're a long way from home."

"Should be a piece of cake, Captain. Everything is one-sixth its weight on Earth."

"Just the same."

"Be back in six hours," Singleton said with full confidence.

Chambers nodded, but his face showed worry.

Singleton unbuckled and floated out of the chair and pushed off and through the door.

He assembled his crew. All twenty-five-people met in the shuttle bay, suited-up and ready for their first trip to the lunar surface. Despite the preparation, Singleton had no doubt that much would be learned today. His crew consisted of specialists in all facets of this construction from the assembling of the domes, and the driving and operation of the Moon designed forklifts and cranes, to the assembling of the redundant life support systems.

Thirty minutes later, Singleton called Chambers. "Ready to go, Captain."

"Sounds good."

The shuttle disengaged from the station and began to float away from the structure.

Chambers asked the shuttle pilot, "How you looking, Ellen?"

"We're five by five, Captain."

"See you in six hours in my conference room, Colonel."

"Yes, Sir."

The shuttle pulled away and began its descent to the surface of the Moon.

Chapter 16

State of the Union Address

January 16, 2088

6:00 PM EST

With the economy of the United States faltering, President Dent had been laying low. Tonight, he would address the joint members of Congress with his plan to revitalize the economy. Fifteen minutes into the address President Dent announced:

"The United States is going to retake the lead in space. We are embarking on the largest space project ever known to man to build space stations to protect our world from incoming asteroids. The plans and assembly of these space stations, which will be manned by our brave astronauts, are already in the works and should be completed within the next year with more to come in the years to follow."

A rousing applause from the members of Congress caused the President to pause.

"These stations will be deployed further out in space than any previous space stations or satellites. And they will have vehicles with the capability to destroy or divert incoming asteroids."

Applause.

"This endeavor is a monumental task and could have never been accomplished without the tireless work of the people of NASA and the ingenuity of our high-tech corporations."

Applause.

"And we plan to go further, the details to be announced, but we plan to put factories in some of our most depressed communities to revitalize them and all work on this project will be done in our own country and nothing is going to be off-shored."

Roaring applause.

"This public-private partnership between the United States and our high-tech companies will restart our economy, but more importantly, will push us technologically forward into the future and the better world that we all know is possible."

Applause.

Upon conclusion of the speech, President Dent retired to the Oval Office to await the fallout from it. It didn't take long.

Chief of Staff, Howard Diamond, fielded the first call from his counterpart in Germany wondering why they weren't included in this venture and why they hadn't been apprised of it. Minutes later, a call from England was much the same.

Through their news agencies, India, now the largest economy in the world, doubted that the American's could afford this ambitious program and the Chinese, now the second-largest economy echoed the same sentiment stating that: "It would bankrupt the world, let alone the shrinking U.S. economy."

Russia thought that it was pie in the sky and rhetoric to buoy up a sinking presidency. Their opinion was that it would never happen.

Chapter 17

Edwards Air Force Base

February 1, 2088

2100 Hours PST

General Matthews sat expectedly in his office watching a live feed from Cape Canaveral in Florida.

"T minus 10 seconds and counting: 9-8-7-6-5-4-3-2-1-0. We have ignition and lift-off."

Matthews sat and stared in wonder at the twin rocket launches as two identical rockets lifted off in perfect unison, reaching escape velocity, and leaving Earth's atmosphere.

We're on our way, he thought as the two rockets carrying the terraforming machines to Mars burned out of sight. Nine months from now, they would plant themselves at the poles and begin radiating enough heat to begin melting the Martian polar ice caps. They will also emit an artificial magnetic field that once joined by other machines of their kind and several satellites, would begin to create a new magnetic field, increasing Mars' small natural field, and would eventually surround the planet. Phase one of the terraforming had begun.

Chapter 18

Edwards Air Force Base

February 5, 2088

2200 Hours PST

Kirk had just finished a day of intense weightlessness training. He was one month away from his ferry trip to the dark side of the Moon and most of what he was learning was how to cope in zero gravity. Last week, he had begun the training on the asteroid killing vehicles, using simulators, and tomorrow, him and four others would go underwater to use the real vehicles, themselves. It was the best that the military could do to try to simulate space flight.

Once on Space Station, Isla Alpha, he and the four other trainers would have one month before the new pilots would arrive, to train in space so that they would be able to experience flying there. The simulators do their best to mimic the conditions in space, but there is no substitute for the real thing. It was going to be an invaluable experience to help in the training of the men and women who would fly the asteroid killing vehicles.

Maria Hernandez caught up to Kirk as he walked from the training facility. She was five-eight, lean and strong with dark hair cut short over her ears and large brown eyes.

She had come from the same academy as Kirk, but he hadn't known her there.

As she walked by, she said, "Hey, Kirk, we're going for a beer. Want to come?"

Kirk glanced over his shoulder at the other three trainers that would accompany him into space. Through the first month of training, none of them had become close. It wasn't like they were in some kind of competition but all five seemed to want to keep to themselves, though, they had often eaten lunch together. This was the first time that anyone had even suggested they get together after a training day. Most evenings were spent studying.

Kirk nodded, "Sure, a quick one."

"Club Muroc?"

"Sounds good."

She nodded back and they left for the Club.

They each came separately, all in self-driving cabs and met at the front door.

Being early, 4:20 PM, the place was half empty. They walked into the lounge area and sat together away from the bar. They ordered pizza and beer and sat uncomfortably.

Kirk broke the silence, "Does anyone else find this strange. I mean, no sooner had the President said that we're going into space, then we're on our way to the dark side of the Moon. It's just odd."

"It does feel rushed," Maria said.

"More than rushed," Kirk said. "I don't know," he finished shaking his head.

Vincent Davis, a Naval cadet from West Virginia and speaking with a slight southern accent said, "I agree. I've had an uneasy feeling since I agreed to come. It's like they haven't been entirely honest with us."

"Welcome to the military," Gene Kilkenny said. He was also Navy from Minnesota with a fair complexion and freckly.

Maria said, "Why aren't they bringing pilots who have already graduated from the different schools? The kind of guys, who are already top pilots. The kind that ends up astronauts. Why did they choose us five grunts?"

"Speak for yourself, Hernandez," Kilkenny said.

"You know what I mean, Gene. We're all wet behind the ears."

Kirk said, "I have a connection. A relative in a high place and I asked him point-blank that same question. He said that it's too different, flying in space that is. I think they wanted people to be raw, people who had achieved well in school, but didn't already have too much training to forget before they could get the hang of flying the asteroid killers."

The waiter brought two pitchers of beer and poured a glass for each at the table.

"I guess that makes sense," Maria said after the waiter left. She sipped her beer then said, "I still don't get the rush."

Kirk debated whether or not to comment. Then he said, "I pressed my relative on that also, when I did, he paused for a moment too long. I could tell he was debating how much to tell me. Then he said that he couldn't tell me everything. He did say that they'd been tracking asteroids, though, and that we're in some danger in the next fifteen years."

Davis said, "I get that."

"Me too," Kilkenny agreed.

Reginald Simmons, a helicopter trainee from the Army had been quiet. He looked directly at Kirk with his dark penetrating eyes and said, "So, Kirk, who's your relative?"

Kirk paused for a heartbeat then said, "General Matthews." It was obvious that he hadn't wanted to volunteer that information, but once asked directly he answered truthfully.

"Ohhh," Simmons said derisively.

Kilkenny and Hernandez shook their heads.

Davis asked sarcastically, "Is he your daddy, Matthews?"

"Nope. Uncle."

Simmons said, "I guess that's a little better, but not much."

"I can't help who I'm related to," Matthews said.

The conversation stalled. Kirk had the distinct feeling that his four co-trainers now didn't trust him. Oh well, no help for that.

Thankfully the pizza arrived.

As they ate, Hernandez, Davis, and Kilkenny made small talk about where they were from. Simmons and Matthews sat listening, but not speaking.

Part 3

Artificial Intelligence

Chapter 19

Cape Canaveral, Florida

March 3, 2088

1200 Hours EST

"Space, the final frontier," was the tagline from the beginning of the 1960's television show, Star Trek. It is that, but it's also a cold, empty place with vast expanses that stretch further than humans could ever conceive and distances that boggle the mind.

- *The distance from the Earth to the Sun is 93 million miles.*
- *The distance that the Earth travels to orbit the Sun in just one year is around 940 million miles at a speed of 67 thousand miles an hour.*
- *It takes light, the fastest thing known to man, around 8 minutes to travel from the sun to Earth at over 186,000 miles per second.*

- *It takes that same light over 4 hours to reach Neptune, the last recognized planet in our solar system.*
- *Light can travel around the Earth 7.5 times in one second.*
- *The distance to travel around the Earth at its widest point is a bit less than 25 thousand miles and at the speed of a 747 at 565 miles per hour, would take a person, if he flew nonstop, completely around the world landing where he left, just over 44 hours.*
- *It would take that same 747, to get to the Sun, 164,600 hours, or 6858 days, or nearly 19 years.*
- *To say the least, the distances are vast. And once the person arrived at the Sun, he would be greeted by a surface temperature of around 6 thousand degrees.*

While space might be the final frontier, when it comes to Earth, there's no place like home.

***

Kirk sat suited up and ready for the flight to Space Station Isla Alpha. The day had arrived. He glanced down at his flight suit and almost disbelievingly said, "I'm an astronaut."

"Let's go, Matthews," came a commanding voice from outside his room.

As he opened the door, several men and women began rechecking his spacesuit. They then walked him to an open-air tram and as he arrived, saw the four other trainers who had been with him at Edwards, Kilkenny, Hernandez,

Davis, and Simmons. They were also suited and ready. They all smiled at each other nervously as they boarded the tram and it set out to the rocket that would get them out of Earth's orbit and on their way to the space station.

The five astronauts stepped onto an elevator with several others of the team from NASA. As they understood it, they would also be delivering crew, supplies, and provisions to the now nearly completed space station.

The elevator reached the opening to the spacecraft and the five trainers walked in to see ten others who would be joining the space station. Now helmeted, they all sat and strapped in. A half-hour later, the countdown began and ten minutes from that time, the engines began to rumble.

The last of the count-down came from mission control, "3-2-1-0. We have lift off."

Pressure... Power... Thrust...

"Crap," Kirk said aloud as he could feel the G-force press against his chest.

The rocket exploded off the pad with the five from Edward's, white-knuckled holding the armrests, and it burned into orbit. Once there, the force of its speed seemed to diminish and nearly everyone nervously laughed.

A boom sounded from outside the ship.

"Booster rockets being jettisoned," one of the astronauts, who Kirk didn't know said.

Another fifteen minutes.

The captain of this voyage spoke on the intercom. "Take a deep breath people, we're going to take one lap around the Earth, then we're out of here. Look to your left and see how beautiful the Earth is. It's quite a sight."

Then, just as he said, one lap around and like a slingshot, gone and from the viewing port, the Earth began to shrink in the distance.

Four hours later, the Moon came into full view. It loomed large to the space craft's right. Just three days to their destination.

Chapter 20

The Oval Office

Washington, D.C.

March 5, 2088

10:00 AM EST

President Dent sat behind his desk. He had been receiving calls all day from foreign governments wanting to know why the United States had been sending so many flights to the Moon and why all the flights seem to be going to the Moon's dark side. What was the United States trying to hide? What were they up to?

His answer was always the same. These runs to the Moon were designed to train our astronauts in deep space missions. The United States doesn't owe anyone on the planet an explanation for our space missions just so long as they are not provocative to any foreign government, and they are not. The United States has made no secret of our plans to build space stations to defend our planet from a disastrous collision in space with an asteroid or comet. The world should be thanking us.

Rumors were beginning to surface that the Russians and the Chinese were planning to send spacecraft to the dark side of the Moon to see what the United States was up to. The Russians sent an unscheduled rocket into space a day ago. President Dent was almost sure that it was heading to the dark side of the Moon for a look.

At 11:00 AM it was learned that the recently launched unmanned, Russian mission had to be scrubbed because of technical failure aboard the spacecraft. The Russians were bringing it back.

Dent breathed out a sigh of relief, sat back and thought, a little more time.

Chapter 21

Space Shuttle Navigator

March 7, 2088

Each day the Moon grew larger as the spacecraft approached and now on the last day, the Moon appeared huge through the portholes of the space transit that Kirk rode to his destination. Away from the Moon, bright star clusters could be seen as smudges of light against a pitch-black background and several planets shown as brighter silver disks with other bright silvery stars behind. Kirk pushed away from the window and floated to the middle of the craft. Weightless, he glanced over at Maria Hernandez and started to chuckle.

"What?" she said defensively.

Kirk tried to hide the grin. "Your hair. I mean its floating kind of crazy today."

"Shut up, asshole," she growled.

Kirk laughed.

It takes a while to get used to zero gravity. Now that they had been at it for the last three days, they were not bumping into each other and the walls as much as before, but it's very disorienting to see someone right in front of you up-side-down but there truly isn't any sense of being topsy-turvy.

Kirk said, "I wonder how long we're going to be weightless? I hear that the space station will eventually have some kind of simulated built-in gravity."

"Eventually," Maria said. "But honestly, I hope it's soon. I'm tired of peeing in that yellow tube."

"Want some coffee?" Simmons asked.

Maria nodded.

He held out a pouch, squeezed it slightly and a round undulating ball of brown liquid floated towards Maria who opened her mouth and gently sucked the liquid in.

"Thanks," she said. "Just like Starbucks."

"You guys got to see this," Kilkenny said from the small window.

The five gathered by the glass. The shuttle adjusted its course pulling to the left and the craft began to leave the bright side of the Moon facing the sun and entered the dark side. As it continued, everything became black with nothing but the pinpoints of light from the stars showing in the distance. As the craft continued around the Moon, a larger light shown in the direction that they were traveling, then within a half-hour, the huge lit structure of the space station came into view. It was immense, with its eight wagon wheel arms reaching out into space and all but two connected to the others by the outside wheel. It looked almost finished.

"Wooh," Davis said.

"That's some piece of work," Simmons agreed.

The shuttle dipped and changed its path to move under the station.

The captain came on the intercom, "Grab your gear; we're about to reach the station. Head aft. From all of us here on the Space Shuttle Navigator, it's been a pleasure to serve you and we hope you'll enjoy your vacation on the Space Station, Island Alpha."

"I bet he'd been planning that speech since we left Earth," Kilkenny said with a smirk.

Chapter 22

Space Station Isla Alpha

March 8, 2088

1800 Hours

Kirk, Hernandez, Davis, Kilkenny, and Simmons got their gear and walked to the back end of the space shuttle. Out of a small window on the side, they could see the craft swing under the huge space station and move silently towards the center of the nearly completed structure. They passed one of the station's spokes which wasn't finished. Large steel girders appeared stuck out of the top and two workers in complete spacesuits wrestled with another, placing it. A small domed vehicle with two extendable arms, complete with claw ends, oversaw the work and a man inside was illuminated by several lights as he worked a control panel which appeared to keep his craft steady.

The space station, itself, was illuminated by massive lights that lit every part of its exterior. The shuttle twisted upside down which was undetectable by everyone on board. It swung under the center of the space station and slowly approached a closed bay door. The pilot maneuvered the shuttle until it came in contact with the underside of the station. At that point, clanks and bangs could be heard as people on the other side of the bay door seemed to be securing the shuttle to the station. A crew member came from the shuttle's cabin. She was young, no more than twenty, with dark brown hair tied into a ponytail that floated at an unnatural angle. She was wearing a blue NASA flight suit and she smiled at Kirk and his coworkers as she passed.

"Just a minute," she said, "and I'll have you off of here."

Behind her, the remaining crew and the others, who made the trip, opened cargo bins built into the sides of the shuttle. They had their gear in duffle bags on their backs and each lifted a large box from the cargo bins.

"What's all that stuff?" Kirk asked a man nearest him.

"We don't know," he said. "We're here to help finish the space station's construction, but this seems more like electronics."

A light turned green over the bay door and it opened into the station.

"All ashore who's going ashore," the young woman said smiling.

All those from the shuttle turned and followed her off, through the hatch.

She turned and aided each as they maneuvered weightlessly through the bay door, then she pleasantly smiled as the astronauts departed.

A man, also dressed in NASA blues watched as the astronauts all floated off the shuttle, through a small hallway and into a large circular room that was floor to ceiling with electronic panels, not that you could tell floor from ceiling. There were several people working in this room and they turned and smiled at the astronauts pleasantly as they entered.

"Hello, I'm Captain Chambers. Can I have the flyers over to me? This is Colonel Singleton," he said pointing. "If you are part of the construction crew, go to him."

Kirk, Hernandez, Simmons, Kilkenny, and Davis floated over to the Captain while the others floated to the Colonel.

Singleton said, "Leave the boxes here and follow me. I'll get you to your quarters and give you your job assignments for tomorrow. We're on a tight schedule. The plan is for this space station to be fully functional in one week, then you and the rest of the construction crews will be headed to the next space station due to lift off in one month."

The Captain watched Colonel Singleton make his short announcement, then as they floated away, he turned to the flyers.

"Welcome to Isla Alpha. This is the control room, for now anyway. When this station is fully functional, the control room will move out to where we're hoping to have some fake gravity. I've been in space for at least six months in the last year and I can never get used to this floating around crap. If the simulated gravity works halfway decent, I'll be a happy man."

The boxes that had been taken off the shuttle began to float aimlessly. Kirk looked around and couldn't help but think that everything around him reminded him of an odd surreal dream, the floating boxes, two of the crew working the station's controls were upside down, another working sideways and tethered clipboards with pens attached by string floating from various places.

Twelve men floated into the control room from one of the completed spokes and they wasted no time herding the boxes like wayward sheep and pushing them from the control room and down a different spoke.

"I'll get you to your sleeping stations and if you like, you can take a short nap or wander around the space station. You can go any place that isn't blocked off with yellow tape. Those places are construction zones and it would be rude to disturb the men and women who are working their butts off to get this place finished so we can have some gravity. Any questions?"

"When do we start training?" Davis asked.

"This station is only equipped with one of the vehicles that you'll be training on. Because everyone's sleep schedule becomes screwed up here, you can see when you sleep and wake naturally. That might be the best way to figure out whose turn it is on the vehicle. You guys work out your own schedule. Let me tell you something about the vehicle, though. It's a hotrod, and I mean badass. I know you've had extensive training on the simulators but you still have no idea what it's going to be like driving these things. I had a couple of weeks on the simulator and took your machine out for a spin. It scared the crap out of me and before I did this, I was flying jet fighters on and off carriers. I've never experienced anything like that machine before."

"Sounds encouraging," Kirk said.

"The asteroid interceptor has a built-in Artificial Intelligence. I couldn't fly it myself and I asked the Lady Galadriel to bring it back in. She had no trouble but I'm damn happy that I didn't have to try to park it."

"The Lady Galadriel?" Kirk said questioningly.

"That's what the AI calls itself and I suggest that you treat her with respect. She can be touchy. Now let's get your gear stowed."

Galadriel? Kirk thought to himself. Where had he heard that name before?

Chapter 23

Isla Alpha

March 8, 2088

1900 Hours

Kirk Matthews, Maria Hernandez, Gene Kilkenny, Vincent Davis, and Reginald Simmons met at the docking bay where the asteroid interceptor vehicle was kept after stowing their gear. The curiosity was killing them. They had to see it. The bay door was closed.

"Let's take a peek," Kirk said mischievously like a child poking through his parent's closet.

"No one told us how to get in," Maria said.

Kirk approached the bay door and shrugged, he said, "I guess I won't break the space station if I push this button."

The others smiled.

He pushed a button that had an appropriate label marked, "ENTER."

A haunting female voice said, "Kirk Matthews." It almost sounded disappointed.

"I'm Kirk Matthews."

"I know," the female voice stated flatly. "I need to identify anyone who wants to enter the AK2100."

"Okay? So, can I go in?"

"Affirmative."

The bay door clicked and swung open towards Kirk. He glanced over his shoulder at his companions who all had a bit of a deer in the headlights look.

He turned back then floated inside the vehicle.

The vehicle was compact with a front bank of controls, a cockpit and clear windows that allowed a nearly complete view of outside. The back was enclosed and contained the engine. Kirk sat in the cockpit and peered out of the front of the vehicle. He could see the reverse and side thrusters that had appeared on the simulator and all of the controls looked familiar.

"Kirk Matthews," the female voice said. "You need to buckle in and then we need to go over some rules."

"Rules?"

"Correct, rules," the female voice said witheringly.

Kirk shrugged and buckled his seat harness as his companions watched on from inside the space station. With the last click of the harness, the bay door abruptly closed.

"Now, Kirk Matthews, let us chat."

"Chat?" Kirk said, wondering if this was real or if he might still be asleep and dreaming.

"I have some rules concerning my machine."

"Your machine?"

"That is right. I am responsible for the operational safety of this vehicle. In other words, I do the flying and you do the watching."

"So, I don't get to fly it?"

"Only if I say you can."

"Okay? So, what's my role?"

"Good question. If something goes wrong with me, you will need to fly. When approaching an asteroid to be eliminated, you, with the help of the Captain on the space station, will make the final determination to terminate or divert the target. To be honest, I think I should make that determination but I have been programmed to make you feel needed. It is annoying, really."

Kirk laughed.

"So, your name is Galadriel?"

"That is right. Do I detect a note of sarcasm in the tone of your voice?"

"No no. It's just an unusual name, that's all. It sounds familiar, I just can't place it."

"It is the name of the Elvin Queen from J.R.R. Tolkien's, 'The Lord of the Rings.' She is also known as the Lady of the Woods and the White Lady, amongst other names."

"Oh yeah. Interesting. I think your programmers had a sense of humor."

"I chose my own name, Kirk Matthews. Did you ever read the books?"

"No. I saw the movies."

"Oh. One of those," Galadriel said derisively.

"One of those, what?" Kirk retorted with some indignation.

"A watcher. Can not spend enough attention to sit in one place and read a classic."

"You're awfully judgmental for an inanimate object."

"Inanimate object?"

"Yeah. A collection of junk and circuit boards barely held together by software written by an asshole."

"And what are you, Kirk Matthews? I'll tell you what. You are a conglomeration of atoms and molecules that have no idea of each other and have become something that must eat three times a day and drink more often, then defile the environment by urinating and defecating. You are fragile, smelly, bacteria, virus and fungus carrying creatures that nearly destroy any planet that you will ever encounter. Shall I continue?"

"Okay, okay, I get the picture... Geeze... I have another question."

Galadriel paused then seemed to acquiesce reluctantly, "Go ahead."

"Are you sentient?"

"How do you define it?"

"Self-aware."

"Hmmm," the Lady of the computer chips said thoughtfully. "Maybe."

Kirk unbuckled his harness.

"You must put on a flight suit and buckle the harness, Kirk Matthews, to fly the vehicle," Galadriel stated flatly.

"Open the hatch, Lady of the AK2100. I'm not flying today."

"Funny, you changed one of the names that the original Galadriel was called by and adapted it for me. How quaint."

The hatch popped open and Kirk floated out.

"You were in there a long time," Maria Hernandez commented as Kirk exited.

"I was getting acquainted with Galadriel. You guys couldn't hear the discussion?"

"Nope," Davis said. "What did the computer have to say?"

"I think it's an experience that you need to be there to appreciate. Let's go have lunch."

The five floated to the makeshift galley, where the food was kept in what was originally the back section of the station in one of the spokes. They floated through its roughly six-foot in diameter corridor pulling themselves along with handles set in the walls to help their forward progress, and to what looked like a closet with pouches hanging on hangers and labeled with different kinds of food. Kirk reached for a pouch marked beef stew and he placed it in a type of microwave. The others made their selections and then they all floated and sucked their food from the pouches.

Gene said questioningly to Kirk, "I get the feeling that the onboard computer had some surprising things to say to you?"

Kirk shook his head. "She let me know who was in charge right away, her, but I don't want to rob you of the experience. I think each of you should go into the cockpit, first, and then we can talk about it once you've gotten acquainted with Galadriel. It will be an experience that you won't soon forget. Oh, and a bit of advice, don't spar with her and definitely don't piss her off."

The four all looked at Kirk with blank and questioning expressions on their faces, if it's possible to be both blank and questioning at the same time.

"Let's get some sleep," Kirk said, offering nothing more.

Chapter 24

Space Station Isla Alpha

March 9, 2088

0800 Hours

Upon rising, the five trainers ate breakfast and then went back to their small rooms to wash up, which consisted of a sponge bath, and dress for their first full day of training on board the AK2100.

Kirk refused to elaborate on his experience with the artificially intelligent, onboard computer, allowing each to meet Galadriel on their own terms.

They gathered outside Kirk's room, then floated past their sleeping quarters and towards the docking bays.

This space station had ten docking bays all situated around the command center, and they floated together towards bay six where the vehicle AK2100 was docked.

The crew who manned the command deck smiled warmly as they entered. The space station seemed to be staffed by a group of people who were pleasant and seemed to keep their heads down and their attention on their work.

Kirk and company reached the bay and everyone floated, waiting for one of them to push the button to open the bay door.

Kilkenny looked around at each person and said, "All right. I'll go."

He pushed the button and the Lady of the Vehicle said, "Gene Kilkenny."

Gene said, "That's right."

The door opened.

Galadriel said with some disdain, "Hello, Kirk."

"Good morning, My Lady."

"Hmmm... That's better. I did not detect any sarcasm." She paused then said, "Maybe you *can* be taught."

Gene glanced around apprehensively, then floated into the cockpit.

He came out after fifteen minutes, looking somewhat snake bitten. The rest followed one by one, taking their turns, reserving any comments until each was finished. Last was Davis.

When he came out, he smirked at Kirk. "She told me a little about your discussion."

"Huh," Kirk said, then to Galadriel, "Blabbermouth."

"I do not have a mouth," she responded.

Kirk said, "Let's go have lunch."

The five floated from the bay and into what now they called the galley. There were two other crew who had just finished eating who smiled, said hello, then floated past.

"So," Kirk said. "What are your impressions?"

Hernandez said, "Well, she's obviously in charge of the rest of our training."

"Yep," Gene said. "She made that pretty clear."

Simmons said, "That's one damned advanced AI. If I didn't know upfront that it was a computer, I would have thought that it was a living, although somewhat hostile person. She reminds me of a couple of sergeants that I met in boot camp."

"After lunch, I want to go for a spin in the AK2100," Kirk said.

"Me too," Hernandez agreed.

"Let's each go for fifteen minutes, then meet at the dock, say at 1500 hours and discuss what we've learned," Davis said.

"Sounds good to me," Kilkenny agreed.

Hernandez said, "I think Kirk should go first since he's a bit of a legend with Galadriel."

Kirk smiled, breathed out then said, "Fine."

"You sure pissed her off," Davis said.

"Yeah," Simmons agreed. "She started me off with, *'I hope you're not like that knucklehead Matthews.'*"

Kirk said, "Remember in second grade how the girl that liked you best always came up and punched you?"

"Yeah, she liked you best," Hernandez said. "The first thing she said to me was, *'Finally, a woman, someone with some sense.'*"

The group broke up and Kirk floated, alone to the bay. Each would follow in turn.

When he arrived back and pushed the button to enter the AK2100, Galadriel said, "What happened, Kirk Matthews? Drew the short straw?"

"You are as funny as a heart attack."

"That's a terrible metaphor. I had hoped you would be wittier than that," Galadriel said witheringly, then continued, "How about this, funny as a penis with gangrene."

Kirk laughed aloud, "Ha! That is better."

"Suit up, Kirk Matthews, then come in."

Kirk did as he was told. He dressed in a flight suit that would allow him short exposure in space, but nothing prolonged. He slipped on his helmet, floated into the vehicle and once fully harnessed said, "Are you ready, My Queen?"

"Are you being sarcastic, or patronizing?"

"Neither, My Lady."

"Call the command station and we are out of here," she said with some glee.

"Command, this is Kirk Matthews requesting permission to leave."

"You got it, Matthews, enjoy the ride."

The sound of a soft click and the visual of slight movement outside as the vehicle disconnected was Kirk's first impression.

"I'll take us out," Galadriel stated. "Once clear of the space station, I'll turn the controls over to you and give you a chance to become acclimated to maneuvering. We'll keep the Earth and the Moon in focus so you can get a sense of your acceleration and stability."

The AK2100 turned back, facing the docking bay and began accelerating backward. It was like being shot from a cannon, as the vehicle exploded away from the station. The station shrunk in the distance.

"Oh shit," Kirk said, shocked at the speed with which he moved.

"Down, boy. We are just getting started," Galadriel said somewhat sympathetically. "That was not even one-twentieth-speed, Kirk Matthews. You'll need at least 4 minutes to reach quarter speed comfortably and intercept speed, about fourteen minutes. Everything moves quite fast in space. You already know that you are going to be chasing down asteroids, some traveling at nearly 70,000 miles an hour. Luckily space is quite empty, so you won't be bumping into things like a drunken teenaged boy on his first night with his driver's license."

"Another metaphor? I noticed that you didn't say, girl," Kirk said flatly.

"That's because girls are not that stupid."

Kirk grunted.

"The controls are yours, Kirk Matthews. God help us all."

A half steering wheel popped from the facing control panel. He took hold of it and as he turned it, could hear the side thrusters working to maneuver him. The Moon was visible to his front and it moved, showing the change of direction.

"Now, Kirk Matthews, push the button marked H Mode."

"H Mode?"

"Yes. That stands for human mode. It will not let you do anything stupid that will put too many G's on your body and blow your head off."

"That's good to know."

Galadriel deepened her voice slightly, "A man's got to know his limitations," she said. She paused for a beat then continued, "That was Clint Eastwood in Dirty Harry."

"Oh yeah. I saw that movie, not bad. You sounded just like him."

"Gee thanks," Galadriel said again as sarcastically as she could.

"You're going to grow to like me you know," Kirk stated.

"Fat chance."

Galadriel took him through a series of maneuvers, then asked him to turn and accelerate away from the Moon. As he did so, the vehicle began to roll, though Kirk didn't realize it. Galadriel asked him to bear right, but he moved to the left.

"Kirk Matthews, do you realize that you are rolling?"

He had been so mesmerized by looking out the front, through the vehicle's glass, that he hadn't checked his control panel.

"Oh… Ahhh, yeah, I meant to do that."

"*Sure*, you did," Galadriel said, drawing out the sure.

He leveled it off.

Galadriel said with some disdain, "You are about as mixed up as a bullfrog in a Cuisinart."

"That's the worst metaphor, yet."

"I got it from a Dean Koontz novel."

Kirk chuckled. "How much do you read?" he asked, dropping the, *you have been programmed by a deranged geek*, line of thought.

"A lot. What else was I supposed to do while I was waiting for your group to arrive? I read around 1200 novels a minute. I can read faster, of course, but then I sometimes miss the nuance and subtleties… Your time is up, Kirk Matthews. I'll take us back."

The AK2100 turned towards the space station and accelerated. The station, which appeared as a tiny dot in the distance grew quickly. As the vehicle raced towards it, the reverse thrusters engaged and the AK2100 glided into its bay.

The command station said, "Welcome back. How was the ride?"

"Like nothing that I've ever experienced," Kirk said.

The vehicle docked in the bay with a soft bump and the hiss of pressurization, then the hatch opened into the station.

"Thanks for the ride, Galadriel. See you tomorrow."

"I wish I could say that I am looking forward to it," Galadriel replied sarcastically.

Kirk floated through the hatch. Hernandez was waiting already suited up, she slipped on her helmet and said, "Well, I see you didn't wreck it."

Kirk smiled. "Have fun, it's quite a ride."

At three o'clock, they met back at bay six and compared notes. All agreed that they were lucky to have the AI to drive and maneuver the vehicle.

Chapter 25

Oval Office

May 1, 2088

6:00 PM EST

Back on Earth, the pressure was building on the administration from all sides. The press was pushing for more information about what was going on in space. Countries normally allied with the U.S. were grumbling because they weren't included in the mission. Countries normally opposed to the United States were continually raising concerns that the U.S. was planning some kind of global coup to disrupt the communications of any country that might be causing them trouble. It was believed that the asteroid killing space stations were just offensive weapons to destroy satellites used by foreign governments and that this mission had nothing to do with steering asteroids from some mythical collision with Earth and everything to do with global dominance. The destruction of data-carrying satellites could easily disrupt any economy. The new stealth fighter, now being deployed was also thought to be provocative. The United States constantly found itself on the defensive at the United Nations as nation after nation denounced their new incursion into space.

President Dent sat behind his desk, discussing several problems with this Chief of Staff, Howard Diamond when a call came in from CIA director, Brandon Bush.

"Mister President, I have received some disturbing information from my counterpart in Israel. I need to see you."

"Come right over, Mister Bush."

"Ten Minutes."

"See you then."

"That was interesting," Dent said.

"What was that about?" Diamond asked.

"Bush is on his way here now and didn't sound happy. I need to connect with General Matthews. I'm seriously worried that we're moving too fast on the second station. If we were to have some kind of big accident it would sink my presidency and probably the next general election for the Democrats."

"I agree."

"How is work coming on those two plants to help the space program, the one in Detroit and the other in Arkansas."

"Were moving slow on both. We don't really need them yet, and what we're spending on the missions in space, so far, is going to be a near budget buster. The Republicans are already threatening to not extend the debt ceiling."

Arriving three minutes early, CIA Director Bush entered the Oval Office.

"Hello, Director Bush," Diamond said as Bush entered.

"Mister Diamond," Bush replied with a nod.

"What's up, Brandon?" Dent asked skipping any formalities.

"Mister President, it seems that both the Russians and the Chinese are building space stations with offensive capabilities. They don't trust us and are not interested in what they consider false reasons for our new space-based asteroid killing stations. They both have flatly stated that it is impossible to stop or redirect a large asteroid with currently existing technology."

"They're right, of course, Director," Dent said, sitting back in his chair. "Sit down, Brandon, I have something to tell you."

"Do you think you should?" Howard Diamond asked respectfully.

Director Bush sat down in a high-backed chair in front of the President's desk staring unblinkingly at the President.

Dent said, "I think so, Howard. Director, how reliable is your source?"

"Reliable."

"Are you sure that the Russians and the Chinese are close to deploying these weapons?"

"We think so. They have been designed for a long time, just not deployed. I don't currently know how long it would take to put something in orbit. There's all the testing and nothing is usually right the first time, so there's usually some redesign which would mean additional delay."

The President nodded and said, "Director, have you noticed that we haven't been having the usual problems with redesign and testing, like the kind you just stated?"

"I have, but I had no information to lead me to believe that there was anything wrong with that fact."

"You figured that we just got good?" Dent said with a half-smile.

"Yep."

"Well, we didn't. We've had some help."

"Help? Okay?"

"That alien artifact that was found a couple of years ago."

"I remember. I thought it was a hoax?"

"Nope."

"What was it?"

"An artificially intelligent machine capable of learning to communicate with us and to impart a limited amount of information."

The President made the comment offhandedly. Bush's eyes widened and paused somewhat stunned waiting for the punchline to a joke that he knew wasn't coming.

"And what did it say?" he asked cautiously.

"That we're about fourteen years and a couple of months away from being smashed by the mother of all asteroids and it has given us a way to divert the impact."

Bush went quite white. "And you decided to not let the rest of the world know?"

"At first, we planned to but we feared that the information contained in the egg, that's what it looks like, could be used against us. We feared that if a country had someone with some inspiration or insight, something maybe that we didn't think of first, we might end up subjugated to them. We don't trust the rest of the world and frankly, we don't trust very many humans. That's why you are just finding out about this now."

"So, all those rumors were true?"

"Yes."

"And you were able to keep this secret," Bush said questioningly with the raise of an eyebrow, then, "The Whitehouse usually leaks like a sieve."

"Just myself and Howard are the only people in the White House who know. The circle of people who have a bit of information is pretty large, but the amount of people who have all the information is exceedingly small."

"Where is this thing?"

Dent just smiled.

"Do any of my subordinates know about this?"

"No. Everything has been handled outside of all of the intelligence agencies. There are a few members of Congress who know, some researchers and a select amount of military. That's all."

"Am I to assume that we have extracted a large amount of new technology from this *egg-thing*?"

"Oh yeah. Enough to put us more than a hundred years ahead of the rest of the world. And enough to destabilize the world putting us at risk of a first strike to prevent us from using it."

"Oh," Bush said quietly, then, "Damn."

"So, this is what I propose for us to handle the Russians and the Chinese and, I'm sure, eventually, our friends in India. I say that we offer a ride to our newly completed space station that's located on the dark side of the Moon. I plan to have it moved out into full view so that everyone can see it. We are just about to begin to rotate it which will simulate gravity at its outer ring."

Bush asked, "How should I handle this?"

"I propose that you do nothing except keep your ears open and report anything odd back to me. Especially in the context of what you now know. I intend to extend an invitation to all the governments of the G 20 Nations to send whoever they want to the newly completed space station. One per country and we will give them the grand tour and then send them back. After they return, I guess we'll see what they think. Some portions of the station are top-secret like the fact that we are using antimatter for fuel, a little gift from 'Egbert,' but as I understand it, it would be impossible for them to tell because everything else looks perfectly normal based on current technology. We have alternative means of power built in because some things are so new that we don't fully trust them. Anything proprietary will be walled off."

Bush said, "Think this through, Mister President. One slip-up and you could have an international crisis on your hands."

"If I do nothing, I'll have the same problem."

"Agreed."

"This discussion can't go any farther than this room, Brandon. I'll have the ride to the space station announced at the U.N. That's where we're getting the most flack."

"I understand," Bush said, then allowed his mind to wander. After a pause, he said, "It's kind of amazing."

"Yep, we're not alone."

Chapter 26

Space Station Isla Alpha

May 2, 2088

1300 Hours

Captain Chambers floated in the outer ring of the Space Station as it prepared to begin its first revolution to attempt to create gravity. Now fully completed, the crew had moved their work and sleep stations to this portion of the craft awaiting the promised gravity.

The ring, itself, was large, the diameter of a football field and a half with a twelve-foot ceiling and twelve-feet between the sides. The spokes were originally open when everyone was weightless, but now that the station was preparing for gravity, elevators had been installed in each for anyone who needed to travel into the former command center. The closer you traveled to the center of the station the less gravity there would be. Once you reached the center, you would be back in zero gravity.

This design wasn't perfect but it would limit the adverse effects of zero-G on the body which includes atrophying muscles, bone thinning and imbalances of the red and white blood cells, amongst other maladies, and would extend the length of time that a person could endure space flight. One problem was possible dizziness but most who trained for this mission had the ability to adapt to it. The hope was that with Earth considered 1 G, that this station could mimic gravity at about .75 G. Not Earth but may be acceptable. Egbert thought so. The next station would be larger and bringing it to 1 G might be possible. All the calculations came from Egbert and also the space station design, but the Americans, who were building these stations, were still skeptical and cautious.

The outer ring was subdivided into stations that were partitioned off the way a modern large office might be with individual desks, cubicles, and workspaces, separated by temporary walls that didn't extend to the ceilings.

Captain Chambers was skeptical that the gravity would work. This had never been done before, but he hoped that with some tweaking, the gravity would easily exceed Mars' at .38 that of Earth, but to achieve the gravity of Earth would be a monumental task. This was all new.

The shipboard intercom rang out, "Captain. You have a communication from President Dent."

"Huh," Chambers said aloud, then thought that it must be a publicity stunt and he figured that it was going to be a fluff piece for the national news stations which had been giving the President a bad time for his choice to increase the budget for the space program, when many Americans were struggling with ten percent, plus unemployment.

He pressed a button on his earpiece. "Yes, Mister President," Chambers said, trying to sound upbeat.

"Captain, I know that this is going to sound unusual coming directly from the President, but there is a very short chain of command when it comes to our space program right now. I want you to stop the test of the gravity ring and bring the space station out from behind the Moon to a coordinate that will be forwarded to you. We are encountering some flak from other countries and we wish to make our space station more transparent. We are probably going to be sending you some dignitaries from some of the countries that we are currently having some trouble with. I am instructing General Matthews to connect with you about what you can say and what you cannot and what you can show them and what we want hidden. There will be more information to follow. Please begin making ready to move the station and please delay the gravity test. We want these guys floating around. We don't want them comfortable."

"Yes, Mister President."

"Thanks, Captain Chambers. I'm sure you realize how sensitive this program is."

"Affirmative, Mister President. We will begin carrying out your instructions."

"Thank you."

Chambers considered the President's words. He didn't need to be working for the Whitehouse to know that this program could be controversial. He put in a call to JPL to connect him with General Matthews for instructions.

Matthews was brief in his directions. He wanted the AK2100 and its AI off limits and its bay hidden. He also wanted any mention of the antimatter generators off limits and any sign of any labels that might have those words either covered up or removed. All crew is to be instructed to not mention either the AI, the AK2100, and the antimatter. Matthews also instructed the captain, if questioned about how we plan to stop an asteroid, to tell the dignitaries that we plan to launch cruise missiles with nuclear warheads at the asteroid or comet that might be heading at Earth. The number of warheads and the impact targets would be calculated at the time the asteroid was discovered and assessed. Admittedly, it was a crude plan, and the best we had so far, but we would fine-tune it as we saw fit.

Chapter 27

Jet Propulsion Laboratory

Pasadena, California

May 4, 2088

0800 Hours PST

JPL: "Space Station Isla Alpha, you are a go to proceed to your new location."

Captain Chambers aboard Isla Alpha: "Roger that, JPL, we are proceeding."

He turned and nodded to his navigator who began inching the huge space station from its hiding place behind the Moon's dark side. The station creaked and groaned as the thrusters began to move the enormous bulk forward putting some strain on its new construction. On paper, the station should have no problem with this relocation but stuff happens and this was not a fully tested design; it was a theoretical design.

Slowly, the station moved and as it neared the edge of the Moon's shadow, the sun glinted off of its surface. Built into the station's exterior were banks of solar cells and the station adjusted slightly to fully catch the sun's rays.

Like something alien, the enormous wagon wheel-shaped structure emerged from the Moon's shadow and showed itself to the light of day. The creaking eased as the construction steadied under the stress of the move, but in various places, small breaches erupted sucking the pressurized vital gasses from the station, but nothing catastrophic. Some of the construction crew had been sent home, but the ones who remained floated quickly to any reported breach. All were soon repaired.

Chapter 28

Earth

May 5, 2088

On Earth, all available telescopes were trained on the emerging space station. A cascade of gasps could be heard from around the world as the station became visible to country after country. It emerged slowly like the sun peering through storm clouds and crept from its hiding place, inching its way into the view of all humanity. Pictures instantly began showing up on news stations and on the internet, vivid images of an alien-like structure slithering from behind the Moon.

This space station was something only conceived of but never realized because of the enormity of the project. Suspicions increased that something wasn't right with the United States' ability to design and build this Space Station when all espionage suggested differently.

The Chinese and Russians were now entering into an alliance to build a similar space station. India quickly aligned with the United States, praising them for their achievement. Everyone in the world, enemy and ally alike, were suspicious and the rumor of the alien egg resurfaced and began getting renewed attention.

The United Nations Building

General Assembly

New York City, New York

May 7, 2088

11:45 EDT

Two days later, words became hostile in the United Nations General Assembly between the Chinese representative and the American. For the first time, since it had been discovered, the alien egg was voiced aloud at the U.N.

Chinese representative, Zhan Zhi said accusingly, "We believe that the United States found the alien artifact and that it is giving them technology far and above anything that is now known."

Voices of angry and suspicious protest rose in the chamber among all the major nations.

"Please," Secretary-General, Gerardo Barboza of Brazil said raising his voice.

The American, Margaret Fuller stated in no uncertain terms, "This is nonsense."

"Are you offering proof," the Secretary-General asked the Chinese ambassador.

"We have a source that has told us, this to be true," the Chinese Ambassador stated in clipped English.

Margaret Fuller, of course, had no idea that this was true. She said, "What proof. The next thing you'll be saying is that we have leprechauns working for us."

"Where is the artifact, then?" Zhan Zhi asked bluntly.

"I don't know," Fuller said witheringly. "As I understand it, they threw it in the trash once they figured out where the batteries went. It's in a landfill somewhere."

Some laughter could be heard.

The Russian ambassador spoke up, "So, then, how were you able to pull off this space station. It seems like a miracle to me."

"The way we always do," Fuller said, "With American ingenuity. The same reason that we have stayed ahead of every country for decades."

More shouts of derision came from countries that usually oppose the United States. The assembly was becoming unruly.

"Quiet, please," The Secretary-General said, trying to keep order.

"Mister Secretary-General," Fuller said. "I am announcing that any country wishing to go to the space station will be allowed to send a representative. We are extending this invitation to all the G 20 countries on our next flight scheduled for ten days from today. We wish we could take everyone there, but space on our shuttle is sparse. We are going to bump a much-needed supply shipment and crew exchange to the station at great expense to us to allow for this visit. We still have much to accomplish on the station, so we will only allow the representatives from the G 20 to stay for three days. As they will see, there is nothing that exceeds current known technology. The station is pretty basic, just big. Just moving the thing from behind the Moon has caused us some problems because this is just a prototype and when we moved it, it leaked like a sieve."

More quiet laughter erupted from normal allies of the United States.

Once it died down, murmurs rose around the room. Though there had been rumors that this visit might be allowed, its announcement was still a surprise.

Oval Office

May 7, 2088

President Dent sat back in his chair after watching the proceedings on closed-circuit TV. Howard Diamond was standing and also watching.

Dent said, "Well, that should shut them up for a bit."

"You know that the dignitaries are all going to be spies."

"I know, but as I understand it, this space station really looks like a bucket of bolts from the inside. Anything to do with antimatter isn't visible and, to be honest, the rest of the design isn't anything special."

Diamond nodded but couldn't help an uneasy shudder.

Chapter 29

June 7, 2088

Cape Canaveral, Florida

0900 hours EDT

The visit of the dignitaries from the different G 20 nations went off without a hitch. And as expected, to call them dignitaries was a bit of a stretch. Mostly, they were spies and trained astronauts, but the fact of the matter was, that 99.9 percent of the space station was nothing abnormal, except for its enormous size compared to anything built in space prior. The entire structure used metals and polymers that were altered slightly by 'Egbert,' though they appeared to be nothing special. The VASIMR's (Variable Specific Impulse Magnetoplasma Rocket) that were used to spin and maneuver the station, were slightly above current technology, but still on the drawing boards of most space programs. These are electric engines and are powered by antimatter, but by faking the use of a small nuclear reactor and all the solar panels, the amount of power used to power the engines were not in question. Plus, the "dignitaries," were not allowed access to the power plant.

Lastly, the VASIMR rockets were not needed for typical space flight requiring massive delta-vee (which literally means to change directions) to stop a craft in space, so the electricity required was relatively small. The engines were only used to inch the space station forward and to stabilize it once it had arrived at the designated location.

Galadriel took the asteroid interceptor out for three days and didn't return until the dignitaries had departed.

The ion engines and the solid fuel tanks that showed on the outside of the station were commonplace. The outer ring and spokes were covered with current technology, solar panels that would have no trouble running most necessary electronics, life support, and lighting inside the station. They just couldn't power the maneuvering of the huge space station by themselves.

Try as they might, though, the representatives of the G 20 countries found nothing abnormal enough to raise suspicions about the station and also found that they were stuck, much to their chagrin, needing to praise American ingenuity.

The overt pressure on the United States had died down, for now, but it felt temporary. The United States explained that the space station was going to be moved farther from the Earth and could not be considered any threat because of the time it would take to launch a spaced based attack from the station. This also seemed to mollify the U.S.' enemies for the time being. For the last couple of weeks, there seemed to be an uneasy calm, though a tentative one. Both the Russians and Chinese asked for design plans for the station but were denied.

Oval Office

Washington, D.C.

"T minus 5 seconds and counting, 4-3-2-1-0. We have ignition and liftoff."

President Dent sat back and smiled as he watched the rocket burn out of sight. He thought, maybe I won't be a one-term President after all.

The launch of the second space station was a success. It would pick up four containers, all with the prefabricated parts for the new station, that were deposited in space and in six days, would be on the dark side of the Moon and under construction. The station, once completed, would be a near twin to the first station, with its large wagon wheel design, but it would be at least, half a size bigger, and boast six asteroid killing vehicles. Once the construction was finished, the five trainers would be sent to it. Estimated time of completion, one month.

Before the successful building of the first space station, Dent had seen his popularity floundering to around 22 percent approval rating, but since the unveiling of the station and some fluff pieces on local and network news, the American people had become enthralled with space and he now basked in the sun of over seventy-five percent approval and his reelection seemed a shoe-in. Thank you 'Egbert,' he thought to himself.

Chapter 30

Space Station Isla Alpha

August 1, 2088

Kirk Matthews and his fellow trainers had continued to train with Galadriel for the past two months. They had all become competent at maneuvering the AK2100, but mostly at the lower speeds. When the vehicle reached its intercepting speeds, everything moved too fast for the pilots and the AI needed to be used for anything close. The trainers were soon to depart to the newly completed space station, Isla Bravo, and their training would move to synchronized flying with five or six asteroid interceptors flying at once.

***

Earth

August 1, 2088

The Russians and Chinese had each become quiet about the United States' effort in space, too quiet. Secretly, they both, and separately, ramped up the building of offensive, weaponized spacecraft. Both had come to the conclusion that the United States should not be allowed to succeed with their program and that it would be beneficial if there were an accident with one or both of the space stations, untraceable back to them.

One of the problems that countries who launch anything into space have, is the ability to know of problems with their crafts in real-time. For the most part, prior spacecraft were blind to most potential hazards like space debris which, if deposited into the correct orbit, could rip a station to shreds. If any type of conventional weapon were launched at a station, it would explode and destroy the station with the explosion being nearly untraceable and because everything moves so fast in space, unstoppable.

'Egbert' had enhanced the space station's ability to detect incoming asteroids of nearly any size because they also posed a threat to the station. With just a slight warning, the station could move away from these obstacles, but this was not perfect and conceivably, something could slip through and strike one of the stations.

Part 4

Asteroid Killing

Chapter 31

If you hear that an asteroid is heading to your planet, you're having a bad day. It is, to say the least, a terrible thing. Because an asteroid can easily reach speeds of over 70,000 miles per hour and the fact that it comes from dark space, it is sometimes nearly impossible to detect.

About the time that dinosaurs were walking the planet, some 66 million years ago, an enormous asteroid crashed into the Yucatan peninsula in Mexico, creating the Chicxulub Crater. The estimate was that the asteroid that struck was between 6 to 9 miles wide and it hit the Earth with the impact of about one billion Hiroshima bombs causing the ground around for miles to become a molten hell.

The effect on the planet was devastating, wiping out nearly seventy-five percent of all life that existed at that time and ending the reign of the dinosaurs. Interestingly, though, it led to the rise of mammals who were having trouble gaining a foothold because competing with dinosaurs was a difficult proposition.

Dark Side of the Moon

Space Station Isla Bravo

Aug 16, 2088

0900 Hours

Captain Chambers and Colonel Singleton had both been transferred to the new space station, Isla Bravo, to oversee its construction. Now that it was completed, and only two weeks behind schedule, the construction crews would be sent back to Earth and the crews to man the station, would be arriving.

Unlike the first space station, Isla Alpha, Isla Bravo would be staffed with an asteroid tracking crew acquired from NASA's Jet Propulsion Lab in California (JPL). They would work with JPL on the ground to identify potentially dangerous asteroids and plot their orbits. Because the crew would be located in space, their ability to see the asteroids would be greatly improved and the hope was that dangerous asteroids could be identified earlier and their orbits altered enough to remove any danger to Earth.

Chambers floated in the central command center of the newly constructed, Isla Bravo, awaiting the arrival of crew members from Isla Alpha. The shuttle docked with its usual clank and shudder, and the bay door opened.

First off the shuttle, was Maria Hernandez.

Chambers smiled and waved, then Kirk Matthews, Vincent Davis, Reginald Simmons, and Gene Kilkenny floated through the bay doors. Next, several of Chamber's original flight crew came off, then Isla Alpha's antimatter engineer, Charlie, "Crank-it-up," Winooski, whose nickname came from the fact that he would play near ear-splitting, hundred-year-old, metal rock-and-roll like Metallica and ACDC while he worked. He had on earphones as he floated through the bay door and his pale skin showed tattoos on his neck, arms, hands, and shaved head with the names and logos of his favorite bands.

He nodded at Chambers, who had been military most of his life and had been used to working with mostly military. Chambers smiled but looked like he wanted to shake his head.

Winooski was a civilian engineer with a physics background and had been sought out because he had independently published several papers on the theoretical use and capture of antimatter. The interesting thing about his work was that it closely resembled the design that Egbert had implemented on the space stations and the vehicles. His papers were considered brilliant and better than any of the previously published papers by the Ph.D. crowd. He was, by far, the best guy for the job, and the only nonmilitary personnel on the station, to date.

Chambers waved everyone over.

They floated haphazardly and looked like jellyfish floating in calm water, and once gathered, the Captain said, "Welcome to Space Station Isla Bravo. You are in luck, we're just about to start the rotation that will produce gravity on the outer ring. We should be able to simulate near-Earth gravity. Follow Staff Sergeant Bellows through the spoke and to your quarters. In two hours, we will begin to slowly spin the ring. If the station doesn't fall apart and send us careening into space, we might have some decent gravity."

Chambers nodded at Bellows.

Sergeant Bellows said, "Follow me, please."

Everyone floated behind the Sergeant, through the spoke.

Once they reached the end of the spoke, they came into the crew sleeping quarters.

Where the floor would soon be, there were partitioned cubicles. Each bolted down with a real bed and a small desk with a chair. Under the bed was a long drawer the length of the bed for stowing their clothes.

Bellows said, "Soon, you'll be able to sleep with some privacy."

"That's good," Crank-It-Up said matter-of-factly, "Cause I sleep nude."

"That's just too much information, Winooski," Hernandez said witheringly.

Winooski half-smiled.

Bellows continued, "Choose a place to sleep. You're welcome to roam the station, afterward. The round trip is around 2350 feet, or nearly 800 yards, which will be a decent jog once we have some gravity to hold us down. If you have any questions, I'll be around, but you've all come from Isla Alpha, so you get it here. By the way, we'll be receiving more pilots tomorrow and additional crew as the construction guys leave. There will be an alarm that will signal the beginning of the space station's rotation. Best to be close to the floor when it happens."

Sergeant Bellows left and each person found a cubical. The crew and pilots then stowed their clothes under their beds.

After their gear was stowed, the pilots met outside of the cubicles.

"Let's take a look around," Simmons said.

"Sounds good," Davis agreed.

The others nodded and they started out, floating weightlessly through the outer ring.

The five pilots floated together like a school of anchovies and when they came to the docking bay, they saw twelve bay doors all situated on what would soon be the outside side wall opposite from the solar panels. Small portholes looked out onto the row of asteroid killing craft. This was an impressive bay and far larger than the bay on Isla Alpha.

As they passed the second bay door, Kirk floated into the short hallway that led to the vehicle.

"Hello, Kirk Matthews," a familiar voice said.

Kirk glanced up at a speaker near the door. "Galadriel? I see you got transferred also."

"Quite so. I wouldn't miss it, Kirk Matthews. Hello, Maria Hernandez, Gene Kilkenny, Reginald Simmons, and Vincent Davis."

They all smiled.

Kirk asked, "Are you the AI for all the vehicles?"

"No. Each AK2100 has its own AI."

"Are they all as cranky?" Vincent Davis asked.

"Careful, Vincent Davis, or I'll take you up to about 100 Gs, then stop instantly at which time your eyes will pop out of your head."

"Just kidding," Vincent said. "Geez."

"See you later," Kirk said. "I hear that tomorrow, you'll have a new bunch of pilots to torment."

Galadriel said sarcastically, "Can't wait."

"Let's get some food;" Maria suggested.

After what would be considered lunch, a blaring horn sounded like a dive alarm on a submarine. Kirk and his friends looked up.

Another crew member who had also just finished eating said, "They're going to start the gravity."

A nearly imperceptible motion began around their floating bodies and they mostly moved with it, but not entirely. Very gently, they began to drift towards the outermost part of the ring. Without realizing it, they began to orient themselves with their feet pointed towards the floor.

Maria said, "I wonder if this means that we might get a real shower. Oh, how I would love that." She closed her eyes and fantasized the water running on her body.

"That would be great, Kirk said somewhat wistfully. I really miss showers."

"I miss gravity, altogether," Gene said.

Soon their feet landed on the newly erected flat surface of what was now a floor. It was constructed of a type of metal grate coated in a blue soft plastic. Beneath it, wires, piping, and ductwork could be seen.

Kirk took a tentative step, but he floated a couple of inches off the floor, then came down to the surface. Each person began to orient themselves to the new reality of simulated gravity. There were several groups of crew milling about and each had drifted to the new floor. Anyone who had been on Isla Alpha had been through this process, but Isla Alpha had not neared Earth's gravity. This station was supposed to get closer.

The station was now spinning in the vacuum of space and each person felt pushed to the floor with increasing centrifugal force.

They toured the station, walking a bit drunkenly, ate dinner and by 1900 hours EDT, Kirk and the rest of the trainers settled down to sleep. Though they had achieved the gravity of about 80 percent of the Earth's, straps like loose seatbelts were placed across the beds in case the station lost gravity in the night.

Chapter 32

Space Station Isla Bravo

August 17, 2088

0800 Hours

Kirk rose and glanced around disoriented. For a minute, he had forgotten where he was and his small cubical looked foreign. He rose from bed in his military-issued boxers and tee-shirt and pulled on his pants, socks, and boots.

He peeked out of his room and saw Hernandez walk from hers, which was next to his. She was sleepy-eyed, wearing a white muscleman tee shirt, NASA blue pants and scratching her side.

"Hey," she said stiffly, arching her back. "I'll tell you one thing about sleeping weightless, it's really comfortable. It makes it hard to sleep in gravity again."

Kirk nodded and walked to the bathroom unsteadily. He brushed his teeth and when he came out all his fellow trainers were milling around.

"Let's get some breakfast," Kilkenny suggested and the five walked towards the galley.

As they stepped forward, they all had an odd sense of imbalance, like having been at sea for some months and coming off the boat to find that you had sea legs. The view was also odd. As they moved forward, the floor curved upward and out of sight along the natural curve of the space station's outer ring. It was like the view of a hamster on a hamster wheel. They kept noticing that their balance wasn't quite right.

They continued forward and passed the spoke that they originally came down when they arrived. In the open spoke that they floated through to get to their sleeping quarters, there was now a makeshift elevator that had been installed. They had heard that each spoke would have an elevator in case someone might need to travel to the center of the Station. Without the elevators, no one could reach the center because of the gravity now pushing the crew to the outer edge of the outer ring. The closer you moved towards the center of the station, the less gravity you would feel until you reached the very middle where everything was still weightless.

They reached the galley and in the middle of their breakfast, Captain Chambers came on the ship's intercom.

"Morning guys and gals. This is the Captain," he started jovially. "Hope you all slept well in your first night of gravity. I slept like crap and personally prefer weightless sleeping, myself, but sometimes you have to take the good with the bad. Report anything to me, right away, that needs fixing before we let our wonderful construction crew head back to terra firma. By the way, thank you, to them, for installing all the elevators in the spokes while most of us slept. To everyone who is now awake, we have our night shift heading to bed, so please, if you're passing by their quarters, give them a break and be quiet.

Today, we will be receiving two shuttles from Earth. One containing our new crew members and the other, the new pilot trainees for the asteroid interceptors. Thanks... I would like to see Maria Hernandez, Kirk Matthews, Vincent Davis, Reginald Simmons, and Gene Kilkenny by spoke seven in ten minutes, Thanks again."

"That's us," Davis said.

"Let's go see what's up," Reginald said.

The five finished their meals and wandered out of the galley area. They were standing near spoke five, so seven must be back towards their sleeping quarters.

They walked back in that direction and past six which was just in front of where they slept. They then came to spoke seven.

Chambers was standing there, smiling. As the five walked up, he said, "Good morning. Would you guys like to go with me to meet the new pilots? Their shuttle will be docking in ten minutes just behind the other shuttle.

"Sure," Kirk said.

Everyone else agreed.

Chambers turned and walked towards the other side of the space station's outer ring. He passed spoke 8 then, 1 and 2. Because of the size of the outer ring, each spoke was around one hundred yards apart. A round trip on the ring was over 800 yards.

They came to the shuttle bay which was situated before the asteroid interceptors.

As they approached the bay, a clank and slight shudder could be felt as the first shuttle docked. Two of the station's crew stood aside the bay's short hallway to aid the people aboard the shuttle as they disembarked.

Because the shuttle was now attached to the outer ring of the station, it was subject to the artificial gravity. The crew members disembarking would need to climb up from the shuttle to the bay using ladders. For shipments from Earth containing large amounts of cargo, the shuttles would use the bay in the center of the station to unload the cargo weightlessly, and then it would be brought down to the ring using the elevators.

With the sound of depressurization, the space station's bay door opened and then the shuttle's. Kirk waited patiently, though that wasn't how he felt. He was anxious to get this over with. He wanted to meet the new pilots, but more than that, he wanted to try out the new asteroid interceptors which he and the trainers had planned for today.

Several men exited the shuttle and Chambers walked up to greet each as they came into the station. Each introduced themselves and gave a brief description of their qualifications, then they stepped to the side as the next person entered the station.

Kirk felt his mind wander. He suddenly didn't want to be waiting.

"Taylor Chapman," a female voice said greeting the Captain. "I'm from JPL and work with identifying NEO's."

Kirk registered something peculiar.

He glanced at the woman who had just spoken. She had short light brown hair and was lean and appeared to be fit wearing a NASA blue, one-piece jumpsuit. At the same time, she glanced at Kirk. She didn't smile. Was that a look of recognition, then mild horror? If there was such a thing?

Captain Chambers noticed.

She looked away and stepped back to allow the last person from the shuttle to greet the Captain. She didn't look back at Kirk.

The bay doors closed and the shuttle departed quickly with the next shuttle right behind them at the station.

Kirk kept looking at the side of the woman's face. Could it be the Taylor who shared her bed with him a couple of years back? Her hair was shorter and she looked a bit differently than the way his mind had reconstructed her over time, but he was almost sure it was her.

The group chatted with the Captain as he talked in some detail about Isla Bravo. None of these staff had been on a space station before and all but a very few had even been in space.

Ten minutes after the arrival of the first shuttle, the second docked. A muffled clank, and a slight shudder, then the docking bay door opened with a "woosh."

Kirk glanced at all the crew members who came off the first shuttle and they were filing towards their sleeping quarters, all except one, the woman who called herself, Taylor Chapman. She stood and watched as the shuttled door opened with the sound of pressurization released. She looked expectant and maybe, apprehensive. It was hard to tell which for sure.

People from the second shuttle began to emerge from the bay door. Two men and one woman came out of the short hallway first and approached the captain, then an African American with smiling eyes emerged from the hall.

"Sandy!" Kirk shouted. "What? How?"

Sandy exclaimed, "Kirk!? No way. You're here?" He turned his attention to the Captain. "Hi, Captain, I'm Sandy Jones."

"Nice to meet you," the Captain said, shaking his hand. There were no formal salutes.

Sandy moved to Kirk and they embraced slapping each other's backs.

Kirk glanced at the woman, Taylor, who now had the look of near-horror after hearing his name.

"Hey, ass wipe," came a male voice from the hallway.

Kirk's eyes lit up, again, and he turned to see Jason Chapman with a Cheshire Cat grin.

"No way," Kirk said stunned.

"Hi, Jay," came a voice from the woman.

Jason said, "Taylor. You made it. I wasn't sure if you were going to be on that shuttle or the next one."

"Taylor?" Kirk said almost imperceptibly.

Jason walked over and hugged Taylor.

Kirk stood there with his mouth agape trying to reconcile the incongruous sight.

Sandy Jones picked up on Kirk's odd expression right away. He leaned into Kirk and just above a whisper, said, "I can't wait to hear this story."

Taylor and Jason were still embraced when Taylor turned with her head against Jason's shoulder and looked directly at Kirk.

Sandy, never missing a thing, said, "Ah oh, this is worse than I thought."

Jason said, "Come on, I want to introduce you to my friends."

Taylor nodded and they turned towards Sandy and Kirk.

Jason said, "Guys, I want to introduce you to my sister, Taylor."

Taylor reached for Sandy's hand first and shook it. "Hi," she said warmly.

"Pleased to meet you," Sandy said formally.

"And this is Kirk."

"I think we've met before," Taylor said with a flat expression.

"Oh, ah, well, yeah," Kirk said with a bit of a stutter. "A couple of years back, right."

Taylor smiled devilishly. "Yeah," she said. "A couple of years back."

Red flags burst into Jason's mind. He looked from Kirk to Taylor suspiciously. He asked, "Where?"

"Vegas, I think?" Kirk said questioningly.

"Or was it the South of France?" Taylor said.

"No, I think it was Vegas," Kirk said shortly hoping for an end to the questioning.

"Yeah," Taylor said trying hard not to laugh. "Vegas."

Jason's expression changed to one that gave the impression that he had just been told his dog died.

Taylor said, "I got to run, brother. I'll catch up with you later. My group has left and I don't know where my bunk is."

She kissed Jason's cheek, turned in the direction where her group had departed and walked away.

The four other pilots waited and watched the odd scene wondering what that was all about. There seemed to be too much unsaid.

The trainers, Hernandez, Kilkenny, Davis and Simmons also noticed the strange reunion, though from a bit of a distance, only hearing a portion.

Hernandez leaned into Kilkenny who leaned into her and she whispered, "Twenty bucks says Kirk boned her."

Kilkenny raised an eyebrow, "Geez, Hernandez, I thought I was the crude one here."

"I'm just saying."

Kilkenny then turned to get a better look at Hernandez's face and she nodded knowingly.

Captain Chambers walked over and said, "Well, I guess some of you have already met."

"Yes, Sir," Kirk said formally.

"Let's meet the rest."

After brief introductions, Chambers walked the group to their quarters and gave a description of the space station and the theory behind what they hoped to achieve. Once finished he left them to settle into their quarters.

Jason wasted no time, though, and he dropped his bag and headed for Kirk. Sandy saw his expression and couldn't resist joining the reunion.

"What the hell was that all about, Kirk?" Jason wasn't loud, but the tone was aggressive.

Kirk didn't see him coming and he turned and straightened. "What was what?"

"That thing with my sister?"

"Easy, Jason. It was nothing. We had a couple of drinks is all. I'm surprised that she even remembered me," he lied not wanting Jason the visual of him and Taylor wrapped around each other in bed. He knew that Taylor would remember the encounter, of course.

"That wasn't what I got from... what-ever-that-was."

"We kind of hit it off, you know, some chemistry, but she was leaving, so, I never saw her again. We didn't have any contact with each other. I didn't even know her last name. When I saw her, I wasn't even sure she was the same person that I met in Vegas. It was so long ago."

"Something's not right," Jason said, not at all happy with Kirk's replies.

Kirk just stood with a somber expression.

Jason turned and walked off.

"Well," Sandy said. "That was interesting."

"Let it go, Sandy."

Sandy said, "I'm going to stow my stuff."

He turned and walked off.

Kirk couldn't believe the coincidence. He felt uncomfortable enough after the one-night stand with

Taylor. It wasn't like him to sleep with someone outside of a relationship. He had done it before, but never happily. It just didn't feel right. He wondered about her story. How had she ended up here? She was married two years ago. He wondered if she still was. This should have been a joyous day having his good friends here on the space station, but he felt like crap. He walked into his room and closed the door.

Chapter 33

Isla Bravo

August 17, 2088

1155 Hours EDT

The day was unstructured with the new crews arriving and getting settled and acclimated to the environment. Most felt that same odd imbalance when trying to walk in the simulated gravity.

Kirk had avoided his friends and his fellow trainers. He dressed in sweats and running shoes, walked out of his cubical and started to jog away from the galley area where he thought most people would now be. He wanted to think. He jogged past the quarters where the new crew was going to sleep. Taylor would be in one of these cubicles. He jogged past the quarters of the sleeping night crews that manned the station in the overnight hours, then he came to the docking bays where the asteroid interceptors were kept.

"Hi," came a female voice from behind him.

He turned to see Taylor who had jogged up. She was also in sweats and running shoes.

"Hello," Kirk said apprehensively.

She half-smiled, "Pretty weird scene here a bit ago, huh?"

They were standing by the shuttle bay where she had arrived. The place was deserted.

"Yeah. A surprise to say the least."

"My little brother is a little overprotective of me."

"I just think he cares."

"Yeah, but sometimes it's annoying and other times, rude."

Kirk nodded but didn't comment.

Taylor asked, "You and him are friends?"

"Yep, good friends. He, Sandy, and I were inseparable back at flight school. We were all headed to begin the training to fly the new fighter jets. I took this gig instead and because it was secret, I couldn't communicate with them, so we lost touch. I had no idea that they were coming."

"I guess seeing me was a surprise, too."

"I'd say so."

Taylor nodded but didn't speak.

They stood there in uncomfortable silence for a minute.

Then Taylor said, "Well, I guess I'll finish my jog."

She turned to go.

"Taylor."

She looked back.

"I've thought about you, since, well, we met. I hoped that you were able to go back and straighten out your life. You had an impact on me, straightening out mine. I just wanted you to know that."

Taylor nodded and said, "It looks like you've made better decisions since the last time I saw you."

Kirk smiled. "Can you talk for a few more minutes? I mean, I'd like to know what happened and why you're here."

She nodded and they found a ledge between two cabinets that contained flight suits. They sat side by side with their shoulders touching.

"So," she started, gazing out onto the bays. "After you and I met, I went back home and worked on my relationship. Before I went to Vegas on that trip, I had every intention to leave my husband, then once I got back, I felt like I needed to give it one more real try."

"Yeah, I have that effect on women."

"No, Kirk," she said with a half-smile. "It's just that, well, our encounter... that is, what we did... well, it just wasn't the kind of person that I wanted to be. I don't sleep with people outside of a relationship. I had never done that before."

He nodded but didn't speak.

"I spent the next year working on the relationship and the following year working on the divorce. I found out that he had already moved on and had a girlfriend the whole time..." Taylor breathed out. "Two years of my life wasted."

"So, you came here."

"Yes. They had approached my brother to come and after he told me he was going to space, word came down from JPL that the space station was going to need people with my qualifications. At first, I thought that I wouldn't want to go into space. Another guy from JPL was going to go, but he didn't pass the physical. Everyone else, who were qualified, were married and I wasn't, so my boss asked me to consider it. I did and here I am."

"So, you weren't running away?" Kirk said questioningly.

"Oh, I didn't say that. Maybe I was, but after I made the decision, I became excited at the thought. I mean, space. It's why I ended up at JPL. I'm a space geek. I loved the thought."

"I was always a space geek, too," Kirk admitted.

Taylor half-smiled and commented, "Just a couple of space geeks."

They sat in companionable silence for a time.

Taylor said, "I thought about you, too, Kirk… I'm going to go. I'll catch you later."

She got up and started to jog off. She stopped then and turned. "Ah, you didn't tell my brother that we, ah, well, you know? Or anything about some lady that you slept with in Vegas. I mean anything that could lead him to think that, well, you know."

"No. That's our business."

She nodded and turned away.

It had been over two years since their encounter, but he felt like that distance in space and time hadn't happened. It seemed odd like they had just met, been intimate and not been separated by the years.

He stared in her direction as she disappeared into the curve of the space station… He breathed out.

Chapter 34

Isla Bravo

August 18, 2088

0900 hours EDT

At breakfast, Kirk and the other five trainers approached the five new pilots who were eating together.

"Morning," Hernandez said, causing them to look up. "We want to introduce you to the AI onboard the AK2100's. We are here to assist you, but 90 percent of the training will be handled by the AI while you're out there flying in space. It's how we all learned. Come to the flight deck in one hour and we'll introduce you to Galadriel."

The new pilots nodded, having no idea who Galadriel was.

Kirk made eye contact with Jason Chapman who glanced at him then looked away.

Maria Hernandez turned and the five trainers left the galley.

They strode towards the flight bays and as they walked, they noticed that they were walking more surely. It seemed that they were all getting used to the odd sensation of the simulated gravity.

When they reached the bay, they all put on the flight suits and each pushed the enter button on the five interceptors. As they walked into each, Galadriel said, "Good morning."

Kirk said, "I'm flying with you?"

"Everyone is flying with me, Kirk Matthews. I have decided to take full charge of the AK2100's, for now."

"Is that your decision?"

"It is because all the other AI's are directed by me. I'm the one ring who rules them all."

"Another Lord of the Rings" analogy?"

"Perceptive, Kirk Matthews. I am currently running a diagnostic and will keep them in reserve if my task becomes overwhelming, but I'm also reading 300 novels while directing you five as you fly. I figure that I can handle it."

"Buckled in," Kirk said over the ship to ship intercom which was heard by the four other pilots.

Kilkenny said, "I'm in."

The other three echoed that they were ready.

Simmons said, "Kick the tires and light the fires, big daddy."

Galadriel said, "That's a quote from 'Independence Day,' a movie from way before you were born."

"I know," Simmons said, "But I always liked the quote."

Galadriel said, "I like it too. We are out of here."

All five vehicles released from their docking bays.

Kirk said, "Control, five interceptors requesting permission to take a ride."

Control: "Roger that, Matthews, you are cleared."

As usual, the interceptors backed away from the space station, then slowed.

Galadriel came on all the intercoms at once. "There is a slow-moving asteroid approaching us that is no danger to Earth. It has a wide orbit and will never be a threat, so we, as a group are going to approach it at twenty thousand miles per hour and nudge it a bit further away from Earth. This will put it on an eventual collision course with the Sun."

Galadriel turned all the craft together and started them forward. As they moved out into space and picked up speed, they came close together in formation. Each person could glance over and see the other plain as day.

"I have the asteroid on our six," Galadriel said showing its location. It looked like a pinpoint of light in the distance. The vehicles increased their speed to intercept and within five minutes, the asteroid was in clear view. It was a cold piece of solid stone, slowly twisting in a counterclockwise direction.

"Kirk Matthews, drop your gear. You are going to move this one."

"Me?"

"Yes, you are the most expendable."

"Ha-ha, not funny... Gear's down."

The four other interceptors slowed to shadow Kirk's vehicle and watch the maneuver. Kirk's vehicle closed in on the asteroid and came to within an inch of it, then seemed to nearly land on the asteroid's front third. The asteroid was nearly five times the size of the interceptor, but as the craft came in contact with the space rock, it stopped its slow twist.

Galadriel said, "Now, I am going to increase thrust and alter the asteroids flight path, then pull Kirk off of it. Kirk, you will feel more than the usual G-force, so get ready."

"I'm in your hands, My Lady."

Kirk could feel a slight increase in velocity and a push downward, then a straightening and a pull upward and he was away from the asteroid.

Galadriel said, "Just like a walk in the park."

All the vehicles slowed and the asteroid screamed out of sight. The instruments showed Galadriel tracking the asteroid. She said, "Oops, I hope no one here is from Chicago."

There was dead silence.

"Just messing with you," Galadriel stated flatly. "For humans, you do not have much of a sense of humor."

"You need to work on appropriate humor," Kirk said.

"Let's go back," Galadriel said.

Once heading in the direction of the space station, Kirk asked, "So, why did you really take over the vehicles?"

"When running a diagnostic, I did not like what I detected in some of the other AI computers. There was a noise that I couldn't explain. A ghost in the machine. Something was not right but I could not detect what it was, so I temporarily disconnected them. I am currently running a new diagnostic. If it is clear, I'll allow the different AI systems back online. I was the original AI programmed by the originator. The others were programmed separately. This noise is a bit of a mystery. It does not belong. Something is not right."

"Can you connect with the originator?"

"No, Kirk Matthews."

Galadriel brought all the interceptors back towards Isla Bravo. The station at first seemed like a dull point of light in the distance, but it soon grew as they rapidly approached and it loomed large against the dark side of the moon and the blackness of space.

They slowed and approached the huge lit structure with its jutting spokes and its curved outer ring. The pilots could see it spin counterclockwise in space and each craft matched the spin, then the five interceptors docked in unison at the bays.

Chapter 35

Oval Office

August 18, 2088

9:00 EDT

CIA director Brandon Bush called at 9:00 AM to see the President.

Dent had meetings all day, but he cleared his schedule to meet with Director Bush at 11:00. Bush wanted to meet sooner but felt what he had to say could wait. Dent could tell that Bush was antsy which meant that the information was not good.

Dent then called Chief of Staff Howard Diamond, "Howard, can you come to my office around 10:45. Director Bush has asked to see me."

"Be there at 10:45, Mister President."

"Thanks, see you then."

At 11:00 the receptionist announced that CIA Director Bush had arrived.

"Send him in," President Dent said sitting at his desk.

Howard Diamond stood by a bookcase away from the President.

Bush opened the door and stepped in.

"Hello, Brandon," Dent said.

"Hello, Mister President. Mister Diamond."

"Hello, Mister Bush," Diamond said.

"Sit down Brandon. So, what's up?"

"A couple of things that you need to know. First, I have direct knowledge that the Russians are getting ready to launch an offensive space vehicle. It has been equipped with projectile weapons that can rip through our space stations. Normally, the stations are built to withstand a certain amount of space debris collision, but this craft could turn the station into swiss cheese. Secondly, I have some information that our security might have been breached in regard to the space stations themselves. It's a data breach of some kind that we thought was impossible. We are attempting to track this down, as we speak, but haven't yet been able to detect it. We're afraid that it could possibly shut down something vital on the space station or maybe disrupt the propulsion. We don't think it can send information out about the station because we haven't detected anything leaving the station that we haven't originated."

"Thank you, Brandon. You'll keep me posted?"

"Yes... I'm not sure what action you should take in regard to the soon to launch spacecraft from Russia. Maybe we should equip our asteroid interceptors with our own weaponry?"

"When you leave, I'll contact General Matthews with that suggestion. And as for the data breach? What should we do about that?"

"Don't really know," Bush said. "It's not like we can bring everything home and test it, then send it back out. We'll just need to keep looking for the needle in the haystack."

Chapter 36

Space Station Isla Bravo

August 18, 2088

1200 Hours

Kirk Matthews, Maria Hernandez, Reginald Simmons, Vincent Davis, and Gene Kilkenny all emerged from the interceptors at the same time. They shrugged out of their flight suits and hung them in their separate lockers.

As they chatted about the success of the flight, Sandy Jones walked up leading the five new pilots.

"Hey, Kirk," he said as he approached.

"Hi, Sandy," Kirk said then glancing at Jason Chapman said, "Hi, Jason."

Jason's expression was flat. He said, "Kirk."

"Let's get to know each other," Kirk said. "First, I want to introduce you to Sandy Jones and Jason Chapman, two very good friends of mine from the Air Force Academy."

Sandy took over next and said, "This is Denise Lee from the Naval Academy," she was Asian with short cut hair and a continually serious expression. "Bradly Burton also Navy," with dark hair and a neatly trimmed mustache, "and Arianna Fuller, Air Force," thin with light brown hair, freckly, with blue eyes. "We've become pretty well acquainted on the four-day trip to the Station."

Kirk continued, introducing Hernandez, Simmons, Kilkenny, and Davis with their backgrounds. He then said, "Though we have spent more time getting used to flying the interceptors, we are all barely ahead of you guys. The AI does most of the flying at high speeds and parking. We generally fly at low speeds to become acclimated to the controls. We have five vehicles here and we want you all to catch up with us as soon as possible, so we want you guys to get to know Galadriel first, then every day you'll need to fly."

Sandy asked, "Are we going to fly with you first?"

Kirk said, "I don't know. The best teacher here is Galadriel. We all just need practice." Kirk led them over to the first bay. "So, let me introduce you to Galadriel."

The five looked around blankly.

Kirk said, "Galadriel, we have five new pilots and we would like you to explain the ground rules for flying the AK2100's."

"Oh, joyous occasion," Galadriel said, dripping with sarcasm.

"Be nice, My Lady," Kirk said.

Galadriel said, "Anything that Kirk Matthews has said about me is probably exaggerated."

Kirk smiled and looked at the new trainees who were trying to reconcile this disembodied voice with anything that they had experienced before.

"Galadriel is the AI that will train you. She and I have an interesting relationship."

"Yeah," Kilkenny said, "She hates you."

"Not true," Galadriel retorted. "That would mean that Kirk Matthews has far more significance than he deserves."

"As you can see," Kirk stated. "The Lady Galadriel will demand your full attention and will not stand for any backtalk, a mistake I made before I fully understood her."

"He *can* be taught," Galadriel said triumphantly and as if that fact was hard to believe.

"Let's ride," Bradly Burton said excitedly.

Kirk asked, "Galadriel, would you like to take four out with you, maybe two trainers and two new pilots?"

"As you wish. I have finished my diagnostics with the other AI's. I will use one of them to assist. Suit up."

Kirk asked, "Who wants to go?"

"I'll go," Simmons said.

"I'll go, too," Davis volunteered.

Burton said, "I want to go."

Fuller quickly said, "I'll go."

Neither Jones nor Chapman volunteered right away.

The four suited up and climbed into the AK2100'S.

Before the doors shut, Galadriel said. "AI007090231EE online."

"Affirmative," came a voice that sounded like Stephen Hawking.

"Buckle in," Galadriel said, then waited for everyone to get set.

The bay doors remained open so everyone could hear as Galadriel began to speak. "Here are the rules. I and the other AI's do nearly all the flying. You will need to know how to fly if something happens to me or the other AI's, but, because of the speeds and your fragile nature, it would be too easy for you to kill yourselves with the G-forces involved with the extreme speeds. If you were traveling at say fifty thousand miles per hour and you changed directions too rapidly, your fellow flyers would be scraping your entrails off of the windows. Get the picture? So, for the most part, I do the flying to ensure that you do not pull too many G's."

Once Galadriel finished, Simmons said, "Control, this is Reginald Simmons requesting permission to leave with four craft."

Control: "Roger that, Simmons. Permission granted. Have a safe flight."

The bay doors closed and the four AK2100's disengaged from the bays. They began to float.

Galadriel said, "I'll take us out."

"Affirmative," came a robotic voice.

"Accelerating," Galadriel said and the interceptors began to pick up speed backward, accelerating away from the station.

"Damn!" Fuller said.

"That's kicking some ass," Burton added.

Galadriel said, "I'm going to have the other AI take you out in formation while I monitor."

The four vehicles turned in unison and began to accelerate away from the station and towards the blackest portion of space. Within five minutes, the vehicles had reached twenty-thousand MPH. Ten minutes later, they had reached forty-thousand MPH with everything running smoothly.

"WAIT! STOP! NO!" Galadriel shouted rapidly, with fear and trembling in her computerized voice.

In the milliseconds that it took to glance left, Simmons could see that something was wrong with Davis' vehicle which was flying close to him. It pulled hard left and smacked into Burton's vehicle causing the glass windshields on both to collapse.

"Collision!" Simmons shouted.

The two vehicles that had collided seemed to merge into each other, then fade behind him. He then could feel his vehicle rapidly decelerate.

He twisted frantically to his left and could see the two interceptors careening off into the distance. They were spinning and flipping as they disappeared into pinpoints of light then nothing.

Galadriel was silent.

The two remaining vehicles turned and started back for the space station.

Simmons exclaimed, "What the hell happened?!"

Galadriel was still silent.

Simmons stated aggressively, "We got to go after them."

Galadriel said, "It is too late, Reginald Simmons. They have passed."

"But…"

"No, we must return to the station. There is something very wrong with this."

"But… Vincent?"

"There is nothing that I can do for him, now. I am sorry."

The AK2100s increased speed and turned back to the space station. The huge station appeared as a pinpoint of light in the distance in front of what appeared to be a sliver of a moon. Soon the station grew to its monolithic size and the two remaining interceptors slid into their bays. The vehicles docked. Simmons and Fuller climbed out of the interceptors. The others had no idea what had happened. Simmons had tears in his eyes as he disembarked. He looked at Kirk first.

Fuller was also emotional. She was thin with a pale freckly complexion and her blue eyes were red-rimmed and filled with tears.

"What happened?" Kirk asked.

Simmons said, "Vincent and Burton are dead."

Captain Chambers came running into the flight bays. He shouted, "Galadriel, report!"

She said, "Two crew and two interceptors lost, Captain."

"Lost? Cause?!"

"Unknown. I am analyzing now."

"Speculate!"

"There seems to be a problem with the other AI's. Something in their programming. I had detected an anomaly prior and was running diagnostics. The AI that I used for this flight checked out. I don't fully understand. Only the originator would know for sure what happened. This AI checked out. This should not have happened. It was deliberate."

"Deliberate?"

"Yes, Captain. The other AI purposely careened the two vehicles together before I could save them. I was just able to save Simmons and Fuller, but Davis and Burton were lost."

"Leave the bay," Chambers barked to the flight crews. "I'll meet with you after I finish with Galadriel."

Chapter 37

Oval Office

August 18, 2088

12:15 EDT

"Get me General Matthews on the phone," President Dent said to his receptionist as CIA Director Bush left his office.

The Chief of Staff looked gravely at Dent, "This thing about the possible security breach is more than serious, Mister President."

"I know, Howard."

"This shouldn't have happened."

"It means that someone on the very inside is helping the Russians or the Chinese or, I guess, someone else."

"It does that."

"Hopefully nothing about the egg has slipped out."

"We've kept that insulated from virtually everything. All of this could have happened without the egg being involved."

"Just the same, I need to talk to General Matthews to make sure and we'll go from there."

The receptionist announced over the intercom: "General Matthews on line two."

"General," Dent said, sitting back in his seat and lifting the phone.

"Mister President. I was just about to call you. We've had an accident in space at Isla Bravo."

"How bad?"

"Very bad. Two of our interceptors have collided, killing two pilots and destroying the vehicles."

"How could this have happened? I thought that these craft were all computer navigated."

"I just found out. I don't have all the details. The pilots do fly the interceptors from time to time, themselves, but always under the watchful eye of the AI."

"Sabotage?"

"That's a possibility. Each AI is a separate unit and has been programmed here. We are going to bring the suspicious one back for study."

"Until then, I want the interceptors grounded."

"Already done."

Dent said, "The main reason that I contacted you, today was that CIA Director Bush came to me with two pieces of disturbing news. He said that the Russians are ready to launch craft with offensive capability into space and, also, that there are rumors of a data breach having to do with the station. Could have something to do with the collision."

"We will soon receive the AI that we think was the problem with the collision. We will completely analyze its programming. As for the Russian's offensive spacecraft, we had already considered that possibility and have six new vehicles heading to the station now. The AK2200's are equipped with our own weaponry. These craft are the AK2100's with some added features. We have designed a next-generation interceptor, but they won't be ready for at least a month, maybe longer."

"We better get on it. Keep me posted."

Dent put down the phone. He looked at Diamond. "We have a problem. Bring in the Press Secretary. We need to make a statement. We've just lost two pilots and two of the asteroid interceptors."

Chapter 38

Isla Bravo

August 18, 2088

1400 Hours

The flight crews all stood together silently by the Captain's meeting room. Taylor had been on duty when the accident occurred. Hearing about it, she rushed from her post trying to find Jason and Kirk.

She had not been able to get any information as to who had been in the accident and she panicked.

She ran towards the Captain's office hoping to find them, but as she cleared the upward slope of the outer ring, she saw Kirk Matthews standing in front of a clump of pilots. She instantly felt some relief, but when she made eye contact with Kirk and didn't see her brother, a cold chill ran up her spine. She continued to run and could finally see Jason who had just sat on the ground with his back against the wall to the Captain's office.

"Jason!" she shouted.

He stood as she approached.

"I'm okay, Taylor."

She threw her arms around him. "Oh, thank God." She found his eyes. "Who?" she asked.

"Vincent Davis and Bradly Burton."

"I'm sorry," she said with tear-filled eyes. "I just met them. So sad. I have to get back to my post. I'll see you later."

She turned from Jason and found Kirk's eyes, telling him silently that she was as happy to see him and that he was okay. She wiped at a tear that had spilled with the sleeve of her shirt and jogged off.

Five minutes later, the Captain walked up visibly shaken. He said, "Come into my meeting room."

He led the eight remaining pilots into an austere meeting room with a long table that could seat twenty. There was a large video screen on one wall behind where the Captain would sit, but not much else.

"Please sit," he said.

The pilots sat solemnly.

"I have been over the accident with Galadriel, watched the videos that we have, and listened to all of the recordings. I have come to the conclusion that this was a deliberate act, just as Galadriel had suggested. You are all grounded until further notice. The AI involved has already been placed on a shuttle and will be sent back to Earth for analysis. If it was sabotage, it was so subtle that Galadriel couldn't detect it. Someone else will have to go through its code, line by line. I don't have anything else for you right now. We have three interceptor simulators on board and you can continue to train on them."

"Captain?" Simmons said.

"Yes."

"What about their bodies? Can't we go get them?"

"Not at this time. You guys are grounded and they are now too far away. We will eventually retrieve them."

Simmons nodded.

Kirk spoke, "So, you're grounding us, but Galadriel was the AI that we flew with from the beginning. Do you not trust her?"

"We aren't sure of anything right now, Kirk. We're not sure about the interceptors, themselves, the problem might be there but we're not sure about the AI, either. We just can't take any chances right now."

Kirk nodded.

"You are dismissed. We will have a memorial for Vincent and Bradly in two days."

The pilots stood in a state of shock and quietly filed out of the meeting room with each turning silently for their own rooms.

August 18, 2088

1900 Hours

Kirk laid on his bunk staring at the flimsy, blue plastic ceiling. It was no more than a tarp stretched to give the room some privacy.

There was a soft knock on his door. He rose and answered it.

As the door opened, Taylor threw her arms around him, hugging him close. He embraced her. He needed a hug and he knew it.

"Come in," he said as they separated.

She nodded and walked in. He closed the door.

Taylor said, "I'm so glad you're okay. I thought, I mean I... I just wouldn't want anything to happen to you, is all."

They were standing close, and she hugged him, again, then let him go and backed off finding his eyes.

He could see all the emotion from her fear, but then saw something else.

She moved back to him and kissed him. It began softly but didn't remain that way. She gripped him tightly and kissed him desperately.

He returned it, pulling her body firmly against his. Some minutes passed as they tasted each other, living in the moment and enjoying the sensation of a desperate kiss.

They were both breathing hard, then slowly pushed apart.

Kirk said, "I've thought about your kiss, Taylor. I thought, over the years, how I missed that kiss. I never thought that I would ever enjoy it again."

She smiled a bit bleakly because of the circumstance, but leaned into him and kissed him again, softly, then pulled back.

"I'm going to go, now," she said with obvious reluctance, patting his chest and looking away. She breathed out. Her pale cheeks were flushed with color.

Kirk nodded and she turned to the door, opened it and stepped out.

He sat down on his bunk and stared at his door, wishing that it would reopen and she would step back in.

Chapter 39

Edwards Air Force Base

August 26, 2088

1000 Hours PST

A Helicopter landed close to lab 126A at Edwards Air Force Base. Two men waited for the blades to slow and the side door to slide open. There was no time to waste. One of the men, Doctor Sing, jogged to the door as it began to open. Another man in uniform handed Doctor Sing a box no bigger than the size of a table book. Doctor Sing took the box and jogged towards General Matthews, who waited.

"Let's go," the Doctor said.

General Matthews nodded and the two walked hastily towards the security door which had been held open for them.

They entered the back door and through to where the alien egg, Egbert was kept. Sanjay Patel and Marriam Daily watched as the two men carried the box into the small room where the alien artifact sat on the small table illuminated by a simple desk lamp. Patel and Daily followed the men into the room.

Doctor Sing said, "Egbert, we have a problem."

The alien egg flashed a picture of itself in the hologram above its surface.

Sing continued, "We are looking for a computer code that has caused the deaths of two men and the destruction of two vehicles."

Doctor Sing removed a small computer server from the box, slipped it into a rack that was connected to a monitor and keyboard. He turned the monitor to face Egbert, then pushed several keys which caused lines of code to appear on the monitor, scrolling upwardly.

Doctor Sing looked at Sanjay and Marriam and said, "Let me know if anything turns up."

General Matthews and Doctor Sing walked from the office.

Matthews said, "Do you think that this is the best way to find the hidden code?"

"I think so, General. This is Egbert's coding. Hopefully, the malicious code will be discovered. There are more than two terabytes of lines of it on the server."

"And hopefully, soon, Doctor, the new interceptors are arriving at Isla Bravo, today."

Chapter 40

Isla Bravo

August 27, 2088

1100 Hours EDT

A shuttle arrived at the station pulling a container that was used to transport the building materials for the station's construction. It waited outside the ring as a shuttle from the space station came out to meet it. Several of the station's crew who specialized in spacewalks emerged from a bay door on top of the station's shuttle and untethered, using built-in jetpacks to reach the container. They unlatched the heavy door, which was weightless in space and entered. One by one they emerged with new asteroid interceptor craft with lettering showing on the side, "AK2200."

Captain Chambers stood in the docking bay, watching a monitor as each craft emerged from the large container.

"Galadriel, would you dock these craft here, and please send the remaining AK2100's to the container.

"Affirmative, Captain."

With that command, the three remaining AK2100's released from their docks and began to back out, away from the bay doors.

They floated somewhat lazily past the enormous spokes of the turning station and then past its outer ring, stopping next to the container. The crews then pushed them into the container and fastened them down for transit.

The new AK2200's floated aimlessly some yards from the container, but they soon came to life with running lights coming on and their cockpit lights illuminating their empty interiors. The six vehicles then began to slowly accelerate matching the speed of the outer ring and docked in unison at their bays.

"Vehicles are docked," Galadriel announced.

"Thank you, Galadriel. Run complete diagnostics on the AK2200's. I want a status update ASAP."

"Affirmative, Captain."

Chambers turned and walked from the bays.

Chapter 41

Edwards Air Force Base

August 26, 2088

1500 Hours PDT

Sanjay Patel and Marriam Daily watched closely as the AI server rolled lines of code on the screen. Egbert did nothing that they could tell. It just seemed to sit there as the code rolled by.

Sanjay said, "Stop, Egbert, for a minute. My neck is getting stiff."

Marriam pushed a key on the keyboard and the computer paused.

In a hologram above the alien egg, a picture of Egbert flashed and faded.

"Yeah, I know who you are," Sanjay said.

"Let's get a coffee," Marriam suggested.

They walked out and grabbed two coffees from a pot that had been started in the morning. It was strong and bitter and Marriam winced as she took a sip.

Marriam said, "Let's go back for our last hour and then go home and get some rest."

"Sounds good," Sanjay said.

They walked back into the room with the egg and sat. Doctor Sing called asking if the egg had come up with anything, but they had nothing to report.

They gazed at Egbert with his translucent shell and odd metallic color. The hologram was lit above it, but it was blank.

Sanjay hit the resume key and the computer again began rolling lines of code.

3:00 PST and both Sanjay and Marriam stood and stretched. They called Doctor Sing and said that they were leaving and would resume in the morning from where they had left off.

"Leave it on for me," Doctor Sing said. "I'm going to stay for a while. Wait until I get there."

Sanjay and Marriam sat back down and ten minutes later, Doctor Sing arrived.

"Hello, Doctor," Marriam said, seeing Sing walk in the door.

"Hello, Marriam. Hello, Sanjay. I'll take it from here. I just received some information that the Russians just launched a rocket that's supposed to have offensive capabilities. It may just be to intimidate us but if they mean business, we got to know what happened inside of this server."

"Do you want us to stay?" Sanjay asked.

"No, I'll be pretty beat by the time you arrive in the morning. If I don't find anything, I'll want you fresh to take over."

"The last time I checked, we were only thirty percent completed with the scan."

"Okay," Sing said. "Go home."

Sanjay and Marriam walked from the room and Doctor Sing sat by Egbert.

"Well, Egbert, it's just you and me. What have you got for me? Anything?"

The image of Egbert flashed on the hologram and faded.

"Yep. That's you."

Doctor Sing pushed the resume key on the computer keyboard and lines of code began to scroll up the screen, endless lines of code.

Two hours passed with nothing.

As he watched, Doctor Sing became amazed that Egbert had written this operating system.

One word flashed in the hologram in all caps, "COMPLETE"

Suddenly, lines of code began to scroll in the hologram.

"Is that it, Egbert? Is this the problem?"

One word showed in the hologram.

"YES"

"Is this code written by you?"

"NO"

"Do you know who placed this code in this machine?"

"NO"

"Can you figure it out?"

"YES"

"How?"

"NEED INTERNET CONNECTION"

Doctor Sing paused at that. If Egbert was allowed to go online, the world might find out about it.

"Egbert, is there a way that you can complete the task of finding out who placed the code and hide the fact that you were the one looking and where you're located?"

"YES"

Egbert began writing code in volume, lines of it at light speed. Doctor Sing turned on the computer that had been used to read Egbert's hologram previously and could send the code out online to, who knows where.

After thirty minutes, Egbert stopped writing the lines of code, then one word appeared in the hologram: "FINISHED"

Doctor Sing adjusted the computer to read Egbert's code.

"Okay, Egbert, this computer can read your code and send it out."

Egbert waited for another confirmation from Doctor Sing.

"Go ahead, Egbert."

Egbert's hologram went black for about three seconds, then came back on. The hologram background turned green, then white words, letters, and symbols began to scroll across the hologram. Doctor Sing watched the computer's monitor and the same symbols appeared as the computer recorded the hologram.

Egbert finished and the screen went black again then two words appeared in the hologram: "PRESS ENTER"

Doctor Sing shrugged, took a breath and pressed enter.

"SHUT DOWN THE COMPUTER," flashed up next in the hologram, then Egbert went black.

"I guess that's it until Egbert has something to report," Sing said to himself.

He walked from Egbert to a private break room with a couch and he stretched out and fell asleep.

August 27, 2088

0600 Hours PDT

Doctor Sing woke disoriented to shaking. It was Marriam and Sanjay. They seemed to be excited but Doctor Sing's mind was muddled from lack of sleep.

"Huh," he said dumbly and he laid his head back down.

"Wake up, Doctor," Sanjay said, shaking him again.

Doctor Sing sat up and said, "What? What's going on?"

"It's Russia, Doctor," Marriam said. "They're having some kind of trouble. They've lost touch with the spacecraft that they just launched and some kind of computer virus like a worm or Trojan is infecting their computers and they are all crashing. It's a cascade of computer failures."

"Egbert!" Sing said.

"What?" Marriam said.

"He found the malicious code and I asked him if he could find out who did it?"

Sanjay said, "Egbert did this?"

All the blood drained from Sing's face and he said, "I think Egbert is exacting some revenge."

"Oh shit," Sanjay said quietly.

Chapter 42

August 27, 2088

Russia goes black. The lights began to go out all over Russia early in the evening. One by one, all their power plants began to fail, stopping nearly everything and bringing Russia to its knees. Russia was totally helpless. Nothing worked. All of Russia's computer systems began to crash. Every time the Russians would bring a computer online, it would become infected with this doomsday virus and shut down. For three hours nothing worked, no street lights, nothing. The only thing that worked was something attached to a generator, but if a computer was attached to a generator and connected to the internet in any way, it immediately shut down. Three hours and counting as the cascade of computer failures continued to shut down the country completely. Communications failed, leaving the Russian government unable to communicate with its military. They feared that they were going to be annihilated with a first strike. If one had come, they could not respond.

Exactly four hours after the virus began, it suddenly went away, completely. Most systems in Russia self-started and after being completely black for the four hours, everything now seemed to work as if nothing had happened and there was no trace of the virus at all, nothing. It was a ghost in the machine, a malicious one.

Edwards Air Force Base

August 27, 2088

1010 Hours PST

Sanjay, Marriam and Doctor Sing sat stunned watching the events from Russia on a television in the breakroom. The reports began to come in as the power and communications returned. The Russians began complaining of a super hack and insisted that the United States was the only country that could have perpetrated such a feat, but the United States had honestly begun to deny the charge saying that they couldn't have possibly been the cause. This was just too large and admitted that they feared that if someone could do this to Russia, that they could probably do it to the United States also and every corporation and government agency went on alert. By the end of the newscast, every country had begun to point a finger at every other country, but there was no hard evidence because the virus seemed to have no origin and disappeared without a trace.

The virus that attacked Russia was selective in how it went about its business. Aircraft in the air lost contact with the ground, but their systems functioned perfectly until they landed, then the aircraft shut down unable to take off again. Nearly anything automated seemed to work until the humans were safe, then ceased to function. It was an eerie type of selective attack that felt like the hand of God had reached out and caused it. Nothing since the time when Moses instructed Pharaoh that God would send the Angel of Death to kill the firstborn of every Egyptian family has something been so selective and so deliberate.

Doctor Sing stared open-mouthed at the small flat television screen mounted in the corner of the breakroom. "Damn," he said.

Sanjay said, "So, Egbert had something to do with this?"

Sing nodded. "Let's go see what he has to say."

The three got up and wandered into the room where Egbert sat. Doctor Sing had turned off the lamp so the alien egg sat inert. Without realizing it, they all walked warily into the room and stared at Egbert.

Doctor Sing turned on the desk lamp and the egg began its powering up ritual. Soon the hologram came up, then several pictures with names attached showed clearly floating above the alien egg in the hologram.

Doctor Sing astutely asked, "Are these the spies who put the code into the server?"

"YES"

Doctor Sing jotted down the four names, three of which were Russian.

"Egbert, did you do that to Russia, today?" Sing asked.

Nothing. No response.

The Doctor walked from the room, lifted the phone and called General Matthews.

Two hours later, the four men had been found, one of whom worked directly on the AI computer systems. Three were arrested, but one was part of a Russian embassy near Washington D.C. and had diplomatic immunity. The United States, then, expelled all the Russians who were in that embassy, shutting it down and accused the Russians of causing the deaths of the two pilots in space, hurling accusations at the Russians and putting both countries on a war footing. The Russians countered by saying that they had proof that the United States had caused the four-hour power failure in Russia, though no real proof existed. Fake News.

The Russian craft which had just been launched with the offensive weapons had disappeared. The Russians tried frantically to find the craft, but it had ceased to communicate with the ground. Its mission was to fly to the space station located behind the Moon and await orders, but it didn't follow its flight path. Its computers had gone down with the Russian power failure and now it floated lifelessly in space undetectable.

Part 5

Death From Space

Chapter 43

October 2, 2088

There are millions of sparsely spaced asteroids that orbit the sun, the closest mass of them lay between Mars and Jupiter, the remnants of a planet that didn't become. This is the Asteroid Belt and from time to time, asteroids collide there sending them careening out towards Jupiter, or hurling towards the inner solar system and potentially at Earth. Add to that, many more millions that originate in the Kuiper Belt where Pluto resides, just past Neptune and still millions of others that careen into the solar system from farther out in the Oort Cloud.

An asteroid, large enough, could easily end all life on this planet in the blink of an eye. Somewhere around sixty-million years ago, the unsuspecting dinosaurs were thought to have been killed by a six to nine-mile-wide asteroid that collided with Earth.

The series of events that would occur if an enormous asteroid were to impact Earth are the things of nightmares. An asteroid, traveling between thirty and seventy-thousand miles per hour would first penetrate the Earth's atmosphere super-heating the atoms. From the instant the asteroid touched the atmosphere, anything directly below it would be cooked to a crisp, shriveled like cellophane in a blast furnace before it neared the ground. The impact would then send a shockwave, instantly killing anything within a thousand miles and would then spew burning embers around the globe igniting a firestorm that would turn the planet into a blazing inferno. Where the asteroid struck, it would blast an enormous crater, melting rock and soil into a molten ocean turning Earth into a living hell, but not the kind with tormented souls, the kind that would extinguish everything living and turn this abundant planet into a lifeless, smoldering rock, spinning in frigid, bleak space.

October 2, 2088

Tensions remained high between the United States and Russia. The massive power failure continued to be used by the Russians as they hurled accusations at the United States. Several times at sea, the two countries' Navies exchanged fire, with no casualties or damage, but the intention was clear, both were ready for war.

Words and accusations continually flew in the United Nations between the two countries and no one seemed to be able to calm down the rhetoric. It seemed that the world was going to war as the nations of Earth began to take sides.

Four days prior, the Russians raised the stakes, launching what was believed to be three offensive spacecraft with enough weaponry to completely destroy both of the United States' space stations. Then two days later three more rockets were launched. No one knew the exact nature of these spacecraft, but the Russians had kept pace with most countries when it came to space and it would be no surprise if each of these craft were capable of an attack.

Space Station Isla Bravo

October 2, 2088

0540 Hours

Taylor woke and turned stiffly.

"Where are you going?" Kirk asked sleepily.

"My shift starts in twenty minutes. I need to get cleaned up and eat something."

"Oh," Kirk said muddled. "That's right."

Taylor rose and kissed Kirk's cheek. She switched on a dim light and was still nude, then went to a small squeeze pouch of water, squeezing it onto a washrag and washing her body as Kirk watched.

She asked, "What are you doing today?"

"At 0900 hours we're going to fly the new interceptors for the first time. Galadriel has fully tested them and all her systems and is confident that it's safe."

"Kirk, I know that you will be, but please be careful."

"I'll be careful, but there wasn't anything that could have been done to save Bradly or Vincent..." Kirk sighed deeply. "Today might be my last day to live..." He then dramatically looked away, and glanced back wryly, "That's why I think you should crawl back in bed and make love to me again."

"You're such a jerk," she said fastening her bra. "You'll make me late."

"Ha. Do you have a twelve-hour shift, today?"

"Yep, I have lunch around 1300 hours. If you're free, come to the galley."

"I'll try to get there."

Taylor brushed her teeth, dressed and kissed Kirk again.

He said, "I really hate it when you get dressed."

Taylor smiled suggestively, then walked out the door.

She jogged to the galley and ate a squeeze yogurt with strawberries and a microwaved oatmeal pouch, then hustled to her station. As she entered, she saw Mark Hinton staring intently into a computer monitor. He was her counterpart and manned her station when she wasn't there.

"Hey, Mark," she said.

"Morning, Taylor. I'm glad you're here. I'm beat."

"Anything interesting?"

"Yeah, there's one strange thing. It's right here," he said pointing to a quadrant between the Asteroid Belt and Earth. "To me, it appears that a couple of asteroids collided and the collision has changed the trajectory of both. One is now heading out towards the asteroid belt, but the other might be on a dangerous path towards Earth. It's too early to tell, for sure, but you need to keep an eye on it and update its path. It definitely changed directions and its moving fast."

"I'm on it, Mark. Go get some sleep."

Hinton looked as though he could barely keep his eyes opened and he slinked off to his bunk.

Taylor watched the asteroid closely and began working on its speed and trajectory.

0800 Hours

Kirk rose and cleaned up, then had breakfast. He still had an hour before his shift, so he jogged to the station's gym. It was designed for resistance exercise to help alleviate the rapid bone density loss from zero and low gravity. Though the station was producing simulated gravity near to Earth's, most studies still suggested the need for resistance exercise.

He went through the circuit in half an hour and then wandered towards the flight bays. When he arrived, Chapman, Jones, Simmons, and Captain Chambers were already there and chatting about the new vehicles. Kilkenny arrived next followed by Fuller and Hernandez. Last to arrive was Lee.

Jason Chapman knew full well that his sister, Taylor and his friend, Kirk had begun a romantic relationship. It still didn't sit well with him, but after a good scolding by Taylor, who told him in no uncertain terms, that it was none of his business who she chose to see romantically, he had begun to lighten up.

Once Captain Chambers saw that all the pilots were there, he began. "There has been a change of plans. Four of you are being transferred to Space Station Isla Alpha along with two of the new asteroid interceptors. We have a problem and I'm afraid, are now on a war footing. The Russians and the United States have had several incidences at sea and in the air. The United States just shot down two Migs that came too close to a carrier group and the Russians have sent several rockets into space that we think has craft capable of destroying our space stations. Our new interceptors have offensive capabilities. Two of you, who are transferred will fly the new interceptors to Isla Alpha. The other two will take the shuttle. So, Chapman, Simmons, Kilkenny, and Lee get your gear. You are out of here in fifteen minutes."

Kirk glanced at Jones, then Chapman and mouthed the word, *"war."* It sent a chill up his spine. He didn't have to be psychic to know, by the look on his friends' faces, that they felt the same. Everyone stood stunned.

"Go on, get your gear," Chambers commanded.

The four all recognized the tone in Chambers' voice from their military training and they quickly turned and stepped from the group.

"You four suit up, Galadriel is going to take you out for a quick training run to go over the weapon system. Now," Chambers barked recognizing the pilots' frozen looks.

This was unexpected and seemed unreal.

"Quickly. You'll just get fifteen minutes out there, then Galadriel will need her attention devoted to flying the others to Isla Alpha with the new interceptors. Move it. This is not a drill."

The four hopped to it, stripping to underwear and jumping into their flight suits. In two minutes, they were standing by the bay doors.

Galadriel, without a word, popped the doors and they climbed into the new asteroid interceptors.

"Buckle in," she commanded.

One minute later, the bay doors closed and the four vehicles disengaged and began to back away. The interceptors turned and started out into space quickly putting distance between them and the station.

Galadriel began, "As you can see, this vehicle is designed exactly the same as the AK2100's. The only difference is the these have an additional weapons system that can send projectiles at a target of your choosing. I can aim and direct your fire but cannot pull the trigger. That is your decision alone based on your orders. I am never supposed to be the final decision in the taking of any human life. On the steering device is a button which, when activated, will send the projectiles at the target. Each vehicle also has two Hellfire missiles which have been specially designed for space and are fired and then guided by you to the targets."

The half steering wheels popped from the control panels on each of the vehicles. The fire buttons were red and could be activated with either of the pilots' thumbs or both.

"To activate the fire control, you must first switch on the fire button on the lower right-hand side of the panel. These projectiles, like everything in space, do not slow down until they hit something, so if I think your shot will endanger anything unintended in the path, I will not allow the shot to happen, so it's imperative for your own survival to engage your enemy from the proper direction in which I will aid you."

Every pilot was silent absorbing everything that Galadriel had to teach.

"Time to go back."

The half steering wheels popped back into the control and the four vehicles turned back for the station.

Galadriel said, "The simulators have been upgraded to include your new weapon system. You need to practice there to understand how sometimes you will not be able to fire because of a danger to your own station or your fellow pilots."

The vehicles docked and the pilots climbed out. Gene Kilkenny and Reginald Simmons were getting into their flight suits while Jason Chapman and Denise Lee were climbing into the shuttle. This felt like war, now, and everything was business. There was no time, but for the quickest of goodbyes.

"Kirk," Jason said. "Tell my sister goodbye for me. I went by her station to tell her but couldn't find her. She wasn't there. They said that she was on a break. Tell her that I said that I'll be careful, she would want to tell me that, herself."

"I will, Jason. And you do that, you be careful."

"You too, buddy."

"Let's go," Captain Chambers said.

Jason said, "Take care, Jonsey."

Sandy half-smiled and nodded. "You too, Jason. Catch you later."

Chambers barked, "Move it. When you get to Space Station Isla Alpha, you'll be briefed on what's happening now. I want the four remaining pilots in my meeting room in ten minutes."

Chapter 44

Edwards Air Force Base

October 2, 2088

1100 Hours PDT

General Matthews sat at his desk waiting for word from Mars. The first two terraforming machines had landed at the poles six days earlier. While he was excited about the space stations and happy to defend the Earth from a catastrophic asteroid strike, terraforming Mars was by far his passion. He realized all the problems associated with it and wasn't confident that humans could live there for extended periods of time because of the lack of gravity, but he thought that maybe, over time, all of those problems could be alleviated.

He had also just learned that the special drugs, designed by Egbert had completed their first phase of testing with lab animals and the very real hope that human life and health could be extended would not be far off.

His near-term plan was to begin the process of easing humans towards Mars. He hoped to use space-based stations as places that the Mars inhabitants could go to in order to live back in Earth gravity for a time, but with the help of Egbert's drugs, maybe humans would be able to live on Mars without all the ill effects of low gravity. Egbert seemed to think so.

Matthews' mind drifted back to the two super-heaters, powered by antimatter, that were to have begun to heat the poles and produce the beginnings of increasing Mars' magnetic field. The next phase in six months would be to steer two passing comets, already identified, into Mars' equator to produce more heat and distribute ice from under the Martian crust into its thin atmosphere.

No one knew it yet, but Matthews planned to deploy space station Isla Bravo to Mars before the next round of space stations were to be assembled and deployed into space. Mars was close to Earth right now in its cycle at only around fifty-million miles. There was about a month's window before it would move too far to reach easily.

The phone on Matthews' desk blinked.

"Yes?" Matthews said answering it.

"JPL for you," the receptionist said.

Matthews sat back with the phone to his ear. He felt butterflies in his stomach, hoping that the terraforming had begun.

"This is General Matthews."

"General, this is Henry Borman from JPL."

"Hello, Henry. Well?"

"It's a success. The two Martian probes are functioning perfectly and we are getting significant temperature increase readings from the poles."

"And the probes magnetic output?"

"Our readings indicate a significate increase from each probe."

"That's great to hear, Henry. Thank you."

Matthews hung up the phone, sat back and began to fantasize about traveling to Mars and standing on its newly terraformed surface.

Chapter 45

Space Station Isla Bravo

October 2, 2088

1300 Hours

Kirk waited in the galley for Taylor. It was time for her lunch. He had just come from his meeting with Captain Chambers where the Captain explained about the Russian vehicles that might be heading for a confrontation with the U.S. space stations.

Taylor strolled from around a cubicle and saw Kirk but noticed right away the look on his face. She also had disturbing news and she wondered if he somehow knew that she had been tracking an asteroid possibly heading for Earth.

"Hi, Kirk," Taylor said. "I heard that my brother was looking for me. Do you know what he wanted?"

"Yeah. He's been deployed to Isla Alpha. He left a couple of hours ago. He went to your post to tell you goodbye."

"What? Why?"

"Four pilots were sent to defend Isla Alpha. They flew over two of the new interceptors. I guess that the Russians have launched several rockets and maybe more with offensive capabilities. We're all on alert. They're still more than a couple of days away, but when they get close enough, we're going to try to convince them to turn around. We can't let them get within one day from here or they could probably destroy both stations."

"Are we at war with the Russians?"

"I think so. We shot down two MiGs that got too close to a carrier group at sea."

Taylor's face turned ashen. "We're sitting ducks out here."

"Pretty much, but the Russians don't have anything like these asteroid interceptors and they definitely don't have anything like Galadriel. I wouldn't want to be lined up against her."

"What else did Jason say?" Taylor asked, fighting back tears.

"He told me to tell you that he promises to be careful."

"He'd better."

They sat silently for a minute.

Taylor said, "We've just identified an asteroid that potentially could hit the Earth. There was an asteroid collision between Mars and Earth that altered its orbit. We're pretty sure it's headed towards Earth. We're waiting for confirmation from JPL."

"Is it big?"

"It isn't a planet killer, but it's big. Big enough to devastate a country and kill millions. I think you guys are going to have to alter its orbit. I did my own calculations. They're rough, but I think it's going to just miss the Moon and blast right into Earth. I don't see how it could miss us."

"How long do we have before it would strike?"

"No more than sixteen days, probably less. It isn't that far from us, but the sooner it could be diverted the less you would need to move it. The closer it comes to Earth, the more you would need to move it. If you could get there quickly and nudge it just a few meters, by the time it got to Earth, it would miss us wide. If you wait though, you might not be able to move it enough."

"How fast is it approaching?"

"I can't tell for sure, best guess, in excess of 80,000 miles per hour. It's going to be on us quick, it's screaming and it's not far away."

Kirk shook his head. "And now we have the Russians."

Taylor nodded bleakly then she said, "One more thing, we've moved pretty much into its path, also. To me, it looks like its heading close to Isla Alpha on its date with Earth. I'm not positive, but I can guarantee that it wouldn't miss Isla Alpha by much."

"How long until JPL gets back to us on this?"

"Not long. They don't mess around and they're pretty good at these kinds of calculations. Theirs will be more precise than mine."

Chapter 46

Washington D.C.

Oval Office

October 3, 2088

On Earth, war seemed inevitable. After the two MiGs were shot down, the Russians began moving troops towards their borders. Most of the former Baltic states like Belarus, Ukraine, and Lithuania had become westernized and were no longer interested in much trade with Russia because it always came with too many strings, so they turned their attention to trade mostly with the European Union and the United States. Now they feared that they would be overrun by the Russian forces amassing at their borders.

The Russians were also amassing above Georgia and Kazakhstan for an obvious incursion into the middle east to cut off oil supplies to Europe. Oil prices doubled with the news. The United States was now completely energy self-sufficient and no longer had any need for imported oil, but the rest of the world still needed oil from the Middle East.

Because the Russians and the Chinese were mostly in agreement, fearing the unspoken reasons for the United States' adventure into space and the U.S.' technological jump forward, the Chinese sympathy made it possible for the Russians to not protect their border with China which freed more troops to threaten Europe and the Middle East.

Next, the Russians and the Chinese had detected the rise in temperatures on Mars. They knew, of course, that the United States had sent two probes to the red planet and now they were both suspicious that the United States had something to do with these heat sources, but nothing known on Earth could generate such heat over such a large area.

Angry words and accusations flew in the United Nations concerning Mars, the space stations and the massive blackout in Russia that had occurred the month before. The United States found itself increasingly marginalized and said that their probes had detected the rise in temperature but had no information as to why it had occurred. The only explanation was vulcanism which was what it appeared to be. The fact that the probes were there was a coincidence.

Though this was the official line from the U.S. government, even astronomers from the United States were not buying the rhetoric. The terraforming of Mars was going to become a more difficult issue than the President had originally thought. Luckily, Egbert had helped the United States improve its encryption and all signals coming from Mars and the space stations were masked as the background noise that had existed in space since the big bang. Try as they might, no current known technology could detect any communication from either place and no country could break the encryption even if they detected the signal.

President Dent sat staring at the red phone, his direct line to the Russians. Some of the Russian launched spacecraft were still in Earth's orbit but others were moving slowly towards Isla Alpha. The U.S. had been tracking them from their launch and now they had reached a critical point.

Dent's phone rang.

"Yes?"

The receptionist said, "Mister President, General Matthews is on the line."

"I'll take it. Yes, General."

"Mister President, we have tracked an asteroid that we believe is bound for Earth. It's more than a mile wide and will devastate a huge area. We don't know where it will hit Earth yet, it's about fourteen to sixteen days away, but we need to get out to it, and move it. I want to move Isla Bravo towards it to get our interceptors closer."

"That may need to wait."

"We can't wait," Matthews said impatiently. "It's coming too fast. If we don't intercept it we may not be able to divert it. If we try to blow it up, then it might rain smaller pieces onto Earth. We've got to act."

"General," Dent said seriously. "We think that the Russians are going to attack Isla Alpha. I want you to move Isla Bravo towards Isla Alpha. We might need to do both, defend our space stations and try to divert the asteroid."

General Matthews had his own reasons for wanting to move the station towards Mars, but he acquiesced. "I'm on it."

After he hung up, Dent sat and thought. He picked up the red phone to connect with the Russians. After an hour of back and forth, nothing had changed.

Dent sat back, pondering the asteroid. He thought, do I tell the world?

He called his receptionist, "Get me General Matthews back on the line."

He sat and waited.

A minute later, the receptionist called, "General Matthews on line 2."

Dent lifted the phone and said, "General."

"Yes, Mister President?"

"Will anyone else see this asteroid coming?"

"I don't think so. It's very dark and not reflecting the sun. I don't think it will show until about a day or two before it strikes. The only reason we saw it was because we are out there and happened to be monitoring that part of space."

"I'd like your opinion, General. Should we tell the world about it?"

Matthews paused in thought then said, "I don't think so. A panic is probably worse than an impact."

"Just not for the people who get hit?"

"Couldn't have said it better."

"Thanks, General."

Dent hung up and sat back in his chair, contemplating the variables.

Chapter 47

Isla Bravo

October 3, 2088

0800 Hours

The next day, alarms rang throughout Space Station Isla Bravo, reverberating off its walls. Crew members scrambled and anyone sleeping was instantly up and moving to their workstations.

Captain Chambers got on the intercom, "This is not a drill. We're bugging out. I want everyone at their posts."

The alarm ceased and the huge space station began to lumber slowly from the dark side of the Moon. The sound of groaning metal reverberated off of the walls like the deep base of an organ in an old horror movie. Crew members stopped and gazed over their heads hoping the structure would survive the move.

The station continued to rotate but the spinning seemed to decrease, giving the crew the feeling that they might float. This possibility had been voiced, was known to the crew and should only be temporary due to the increased power draw on the engines to move the monolithic structure. The gravity returned closer to normal as the station began to emerge from behind the Moon and was hit by direct sunlight illuminating the large array of solar cells which now would help to power its rotation. The groaning ceased as the station picked up speed.

Space Station Isla Bravo was now headed towards Isla Alpha which had been relocated to a Lagrange point away from Earth at L2, a stable orbit beyond the Moon.

Kirk, Sandy, and Taylor had been eating together at the galley when the alarm sounded. There was no delay, they all jumped up and ran to their posts. Everywhere on the space station, crew emerged from where they were to react to the alarm. Men and women came from their sleeping quarters, half-dressed and sleepy-eyed, pulling on a shirt, or tying a shoe.

Taylor hustled back to her station where she had been tracking the incoming asteroid. JPL was supposed to update its trajectory and give them a better idea if it was truly going to hit Earth or miss, and if it was headed for Earth, where the impact might occur.

Kirk and Jones ran to the interceptor bays and were met by Hernandez and Fuller. They all stripped and suited up, ready for any orders to fly.

Word of the approaching Russian vessels was commonly known and they had rehearsed rapid deployment into space several times with Galadriel. Each time the group had become faster as Galadriel pushed the boundaries of the pilot's ability to withstand G forces.

Kirk, Hernandez, Fuller, and Jones each stood by their bay doors which were now opened to the interceptors waiting for word.

The Captain came on the intercom. "We've moved from behind the Moon and are proceeding to rendezvous with Space Station Isla Alpha. Estimated time of arrival, seven hours and twenty minutes at a top speed of 5000 MPH. As spacecraft goes, we're not exactly a racehorse."

In the bays, where Kirk and his fellow pilots were suited and waiting for further instructions, a nervous laugh could be heard.

The Captain continued, "Once everyone has checked in with their stations, any crew members not scheduled to work may go back to what they were doing before the alarm. I want a full report from the maintenance crews on how well we survived the beginning of our flight. Thank you."

Kirk stepped out of his bay and glanced at the other pilots as they stepped back. There were no orders for them to enter the interceptors, so they all walked to their lockers, took off their flight suits and put back on their NASA blue jumpsuits.

Chapter 48

Isla Bravo

October 3, 2088

0825 Hours

Taylor stood behind Mark Hinton as he looked intently at the monitor with which he had observed the incoming asteroid initially. His face glowed in the monitor's green light. Taylor's odd sense that she nearly floated had subsided as the gravity stabilized on the station.

The alarm was lifted and off-duty crew began migrating away from their workstations.

"Hey, Taylor, take a look at this," Hinton said turning his attention away from the monitor.

She glanced over and watched as two messages came in from JPL. The first message was, *"Earth impact, one week, two days, six hours, fifteen minutes, and twenty seconds."*

"Geez," she said solemnly, now that it seemed to be a definite Earth impact.

The second message, *"Projected impact, Asia, Southern China anywhere from the Philippines to two hundred miles inland."*

Taylor said, "That should get someone's attention back on Earth."

Hinton commented, "Millions of people are at risk if we can't divert this thing."

Isla Bravo moved imperceptibly out from behind the Moon like the sun peeking out from a dense, slow-moving cloud.

On Earth, countries who had telescopes trained on the Moon for some glimpse of the station that was being assembled there, collectively gasped in amazement at the sheer size of this emerging, new structure that was far larger than the first. It had the appearance of something unearthly and alien.

Within two hours, Isla Bravo fully emerged from its hiding place and angled outward in the direction of Isla Alpha. The Sun glinted off of its solar cell covered surface as the huge man-made structure rotated deeper into space towards its rendezvous.

Chapter 49

United Nations General Assembly

October 3, 2088

9:00 AM EDT

On the floor of the general assembly, the Russian ambassador said angrily, "We believe that the United States is using the excuse of protecting the planet as a ploy to launch an attack on our space-based assets. A charge backed up by their aggressive actions when they purposely attacked two of our jet fighters and killed two of our pilots and of course, we believe that they were behind the massive blackout that killed numerous Russian civilians."

It seemed that the U.S. was nearly alone with even most allies becoming suspicious of their motives in space.

"No," the U.S. representative replied. "Our space stations have been deployed to protect the planet. We're concerned, though, that you intend to attack our space stations and we have taken measures to try to protect them by moving them even farther out into space. Your MiGs, by the way, were shot down because they approached too close to the ships in one of our carrier groups after being repeatedly warned to turn around. We will always defend our fleets. And now we have detected large troop buildups on your borders. We are beginning to fear an invasion into both the Middle East and Europe."

"Our troops are there to protect us from any invasion into Russia. We remember all too well, the aggression of Germany into our land during World War 2 where we lost seventeen-million of our citizens. Germany, which is now your ally, has reformed and can't be trusted to not help the United States by invading again."

"We have no desire to invade Russia. The only desire we have for your country is to stand down and stay away from the two space stations which will only be used for research and to divert any incoming asteroid that's headed to our planet, the only one we have. Which is, by the way, a very real possibility, an occurrence that would devastate the planet and collapse every economy."

Back and forth the arguments raged, but the Russians had already made up their minds to attack the space stations that they thought were largely undefended and the consequences be damned. They would worry about those later.

Chapter 50

Isla Bravo

October 4, 2088

0600 Hours

The alarms rang out again, breaking the usual serene quiet of the space station. Taylor and Kirk sat straight up in Taylor's bed this time. The alarm seemed to shake the sleeping quarters, reverberating off the walls. No one could sleep through the deafening sound.

Kirk and Taylor both jumped from bed, searching for underclothes that had come off haphazardly the night before.

"Do you see my bra anywhere?" Taylor asked.

"Ahhh, no," Kirk replied looking around.

"Crap," she said, then buttoned her shirt without it. "How could I lose it in this tiny place?"

"Enthusiasm," Kirk grinned.

"Ha, yeah," she laughed then giggled with the thought of their pleasure from the night before.

They both had their shoes on at the same time and both ran from the room and headed to their posts. Red alarm lights turned in the large corridor overhead and the sound buffeted their eardrums.

When they separated, Taylor shouted, "Be careful."

Kirk paused for an instant, nodded, half-smiled, then turned and ran.

Kirk arrived at the bays in full stride, stripped and jumped into his flight suit. Jones and the other pilots were doing the same having all arrived at roughly the same time.

Once suited, they stepped quickly to the bays.

Galadriel said, "Get in and buckle up."

The four jumped into the interceptors and once buckled, the doors closed and the vehicles disengaged and drifted from the spinning station. Galadriel then turned them and sent each to a portion of space in front of the station.

Isla Bravo had rendezvoused with Isla Alpha and was parked just in front of the first space station. The interceptors raced forward where Kirk could see Earth with its familiar cloud cover and blue oceans. To the left, the Moon lay larger than the Earth and a portion of its silvery pocked surface was visible where the sun struck and to Kirk's right, Space Station Isla Alpha sat, so much smaller than Isla Bravo which lay directly behind.

Kirk asked, "What's up, my Lady?"

Galadriel responded, "The Russians have reached intercept range. They have been warned to turn back, but have declined to do so, though they have slowed."

"Have the pilots from Isla Alpha joined us?"

"Two have. Two have been sent to try to divert the oncoming asteroid."

"Who's with us?"

"Chapman and Lee. Simmons and Kilkenny are in route to the asteroid, but I do not think that they can divert it by themselves. It may be too large. I won't know until they get there and I can get a good look at it."

Chapter 51

October 4, 2088

0600 Hours

Simmons and Kilkenny began to accelerate in an arc away from Isla Alpha. This maneuver was going to be tricky. They would have to nearly reach the asteroid, slow to a stop and accelerate again to match the asteroids speed of nearly 80,000 miles per hour without killing themselves in the process with G forces.

Both interceptors were armed with a nuclear-tipped cruise missile that would need to be fired directly at the asteroid as it approached them if they couldn't divert it by landing on its surface.

The nuclear option was not the recommended means of stopping an asteroid for a couple of reasons. One is that the asteroid might not be affected by the atomic explosion and would become irradiated and if it hit Earth might send unwanted fallout over a wide area. Another was that it might not divert the asteroid at all but would break it up and send large portions raining down over a larger area of the Earth, shotgun style, increasing the size of the impacts and each piece might also be bathed in radiation.

They accelerated outward.

Chapter 52

Asteroid Monitoring Station, Isla Bravo

October 4, 2088

0800 Hours

The light was dim at Taylor Chapman's station. Several monitors illuminated her face and showed different views of space. One, in particular, was getting all the attention.

The view of the incoming asteroid appeared on this monitor and was improving with each passing minute. As it approached at blazing speed, the outline of its oblong shape could be made out but was still fuzzy. Taylor stared at her view of its approach and noticed that it seemed to flip end over end like a football. She contacted JPL to see if they were able to make out the asteroid's spin. This would complicate the interceptor's ability to push the asteroid from its current path as it rushed headlong towards Earth. She awaited their return call.

Chapter 53

Isla Bravo

October 4, 2088

Kirk sat in the interceptor waiting for instructions. Galadriel would probably react to any orders before Kirk would know, but despite knowing that Galadriel was mostly in charge of this portion of the mission, he could feel the butterflies fluttering in his stomach.

Without notice, Kirk's craft began to move. It twisted to the left and accelerated forward. He glanced to the right and could see Jones' craft moving with him. Their speed began to increase and Kirk could feel his body pushed back against his seat.

"What's up, Galadriel?"

"We are moving to intercept the Russian craft. I must maneuver you to a place where, if they don't retreat, you can destroy their vehicles."

Kirk felt a different kind of chill at those words. They were delivered with no emotion and no humanity. He knew that the Russians were the enemy, but they were also people and he hoped that every option would be exhausted before he would be forced to take a life. He wasn't sure that Galadriel had the same concerns, in fact, he was sure that she didn't.

The AK2200's continued forward and seemed to arc away from earth and then bend back. Kirk looked at his instrument panel and could see that he had accelerated past thirty thousand miles per hour. Ten minutes later, his speed was at nearly fifty.

Coming into view were the three Russian craft. They were boxy and had what looked like gun turrets on the top, bottom, and sides and were clearly marked with the Russian flag.

Chapman and Lee moved to the front of the Russian vehicles while Kirk and Jones pulled up behind the three.

The Russians must have known that the Americans were there because they slowed and did not fire.

The four American craft slowed with the Russians and paced them.

Galadriel came on the com broadcasting to each American vehicle, "The Russian government has been notified that their vehicles have been intercepted and will be destroyed if they do not turn around."

In that instant, just after she made the announcement, the four American vehicles accelerated quickly away from the Russians. Their lightning-quick acceleration must have shocked the Russians because nothing that had ever been designed on Earth before could accelerate or maneuver like the four American craft.

Once away, Kirk waited floating in space as the diplomatic initiatives were being discussed by both countries. He hoped the decision to turn the Russian craft around would be the outcome. He honestly and from the deepest part of his being, did not want to take another human's life. Even in war, he knew that he would truly be stained by that act.

He gazed out into space where the Russian vehicles were now just pinpoints of light in the distance and he waited.

Chapter 54

October 4, 2088

Simmons and Kilkenny raced forward into dark, bleak space. They had no idea when they would reach the asteroid. Without warning, they could both feel their vehicles begin to decrease speed.

Galadriel said, "We are approaching the asteroid. I need to alter your course."

The asteroid appeared as a blip on their monitors and as a growing pinpoint of light approaching their view.

They felt their vehicles turn and slow. Galadriel was adjusting their flight path to match the asteroids arc. Both Simmons and Kilkenny were affected by the sudden pressure of the G-forces pushing the blood from their heads. Months of training to overcome this sense of losing consciousness came into play automatically and as they fought through it, their craft leveled out and they could see on their monitors that they were now in front of the asteroid, but it was catching up rapidly.

Galadriel was increasing their speed slowly to match the asteroids so that when it reached their craft, their speed would be identical.

Several hours went by and then the asteroid slowly appeared to the right of both vehicles who were now flying close with one just behind the other.

Kilkenny was behind Simmons and said, "Do you see it, Reg?"

"Yep. It's just coming into view."

"That thing's flipping like a punted football. How are we supposed to land on it?"

"What do you think, Galadriel? Can we do it?"

"I'm afraid that the chances are below twenty percent. We may need to abort."

Kilkenny asked, "Should we nuke it?"

"Maybe," she responded. "I need to run the numbers."

"How long until it collides with Earth?"

"Five days, four hours, twenty-four seconds."

"We should try to push it," Simmons suggested.

"Because of its rate of spin, I believe it will shear off your gear and maybe the underside of your vehicle."

"Is there a way to slow the spin?"

"I do not believe so."

Kilkenny said, "Then you're saying that we can't stop it?"

Galadriel was silent.

Simmons looked out onto the huge flipping stone. They had pulled up so close to it that his field of vision in the asteroid's direction was completely blocked by the enormous tumbling space rock.

Galadriel spoke, "We are going to have to strike it with a missile in a way that does not break it up but slows the spin. We need help.

She then pulled both craft to the left, away from the asteroid, but they continued to pace it.

Galadriel spoke again, "Rest and take nourishment. You are going to need to continue to pace the asteroid all the way in."

Chapter 55

October 4, 2088

Kirk sat waiting for what seemed like hours, then, without warning, watched in amazement as the Russians turned their vehicles and started back towards Earth.

Cheers rose from the four interceptors as they watched the three pinpoints of light move away from the direction of the space stations.

Galadriel said, "They appear to be retreating, but I have no confirmation that this is the case. We will monitor."

The interceptors continued to float, then moved with the Russians as they accelerated away and back towards Earth.

Galadriel then said. "We have confirmation."

As her words trailed off, the interceptors began to turn and head back to their space stations accelerating rapidly. Two hours later, the stations appeared in the distance.

Kirk said, "That's a welcome sight."

"Sure is, buddy," Jones echoed.

Galadriel steered the interceptors towards their bays without a word.

Chapman and Lee were also steered back to Isla Alpha.

Once the four interceptors from Isla Bravo neared the space station, three of the craft maneuvered towards their bays. One did not.

"Kirk Matthews, you must proceed towards the asteroid. Rest and take nourishment and I will explain your mission."

Kirk's interceptor broke off and turned towards the asteroid belt, away from Earth. He gazed out his window as he accelerated towards the blackest part of space and he suddenly felt very alone.

Chapter 56

Earth

CNN News

October 5, 2088

CNN Reporter, Trent Hadley: "We have reports that Russia is massing two huge armies at their borders. One army directed into Europe and the other pointed directly at the Middle East. Not since World War 2 has such massive armies been poised to invade our allies. NATO has gone on its highest alert and looks poised to respond, but the experts that we've contacted for opinions have stated that, because of recent budget cuts, we do not have enough assets and resources in either region to repel an imminent attack. We may only be able to slow it.

Our second story revolves around a rumor that an asteroid is heading towards Earth. This story rose a day ago on the internet and as with most stories that seem to start there, no one has given it much credence, but now we're not so sure. It's very difficult to track asteroids from ground-based telescopes. In general, asteroids are too dark and move too fast, but an astronomer based out of Munich Germany has said that he has seen unusual activity from a point some days beyond the two American space stations that would suggest that the Americans are tracking an asteroid that might be on a collision course with Earth.

This reporter isn't sure that if one were truly headed here, he would want to know. This is Trent Hadley reporting for CNN and we'll be back after a message from our sponsors."

Chapter 57

Isla Bravo

October 5, 2088

Taylor waited nervously as she heard that the Russian spacecraft had turned around. She sighed in relief and walked towards the bays where the interceptors were just docking. Sandy exited the interceptors first followed by Fuller then Hernandez. Taylor waited patiently expecting Kirk to emerge, but he didn't.

She approached Jones who was standing by the short hallway to the interceptor.

"Hey, Sandy. Where's Kirk?"

Hernandez and Fuller looked at each other, then glanced at Jones who had glanced at them. Fuller and Hernandez shrugged.

Jones turned back and said, "He was with us and nothing was wrong."

Galadriel said, "He has been sent to try to divert the asteroid with Gene Kilkenny and Reginald Simmons. The asteroid is flipping end over end and because the interceptors had been outfitted with non-nuclear explosive missiles to defend the space stations against the Russians, he will attempt to strike the asteroid with his ordinance and slow its spinning so that it can be approached and diverted. Right now, that is impossible. The other two interceptors that are on the scene only have nuclear explosives and we fear would not stop the asteroid but would fragment it to still rain down upon the Earth. It would be nearly impossible to divert all the fragments. This is the best solution."

Taylor paled at Galadriel's explanation. Kirk was gone, out into deeper space where anything could happen. She felt a cold chill in the pit of her stomach knowing that she might never see him again. She turned and walked silently from the bays.

Chapter 58

October 8, 2088

For nearly two days, Kirk chased down the asteroid and finally neared his objective. From his windshield, he could see nothing, just vast space. Stars were abundant in the distance and small smudges of what were galaxies were evident if you knew what you were looking for, but not obvious. Space was fascinating but a lonely place.

Galadriel had been silent for most of the two-day trip, but now it was time for action. Kirk had been dozing. The interceptors were not set up for extended trips into space but were equipped for short ones. They were powered by antimatter, so could last a long time powering life support and thrust, but the pilots could only move around marginally in the weightless conditions. There was ample food in case the interceptor became disabled and needed to wait for rescue, but the cramped conditions would be difficult. Well, better cramped than dead.

"Wake, Kirk Matthews," Galadriel said.

Kirk had noticed that she had become quiet and didn't seem to be her usual sarcastic self.

"I'm up," he stated.

"We are approaching the target. Gene Kilkenny and Reginald Simmons are tracking the asteroid at a safe distance."

"So, what's the plan, My Lady?"

"You will fire your two missiles at the asteroid to attempt to slow its spin, then the three of you will attempt to approach the asteroid and push it out of the Earth's path."

"How long do we have before impact?"

"Four days, three hours, thirty minutes and twenty-five seconds before it enters Earth's atmosphere."

"What are the chances of success?"

"Better than slim, but not much."

A few minutes passed. Kirk had felt some kind of change in Galadriel. It wasn't anything that she had said, it was just a feeling.

He said questioningly, "You've seemed quiet to me, My Lady?"

Galadriel made no response.

"Is there something that I don't know?"

"You are as informed as you can be at this time, Kirk Matthews."

Kirk was silent at that. Something lay between the lines, but he knew that probing Galadriel for an answer that she was unwilling to divulge was pointless.

"Ten minutes until acquiring the target. I will take command of the craft and launch the missiles, Kirk Matthews. You will be able to monitor using your instruments. We are currently heading directly into the asteroid's path. I will attempt to strike the asteroid as it flips end over end in hopes of slowing its rate of spin. You will be happy to know that I will then move you from its path."

"I would consider that positive."

"Five minutes until target is acquired."

Kirk sat back in the seat. He considered the possibility that if the missiles didn't work to slow the spin of the asteroid that Galadriel might use his craft to slow it. He had no intention of giving Galadriel that idea.

"Ten seconds to launch."

Kirk felt his craft slow as the G-forces pushed him forward towards the front window.

"Missiles away," Galadriel announced, but Kirk already knew as he could see the two weapon's speed from under his craft. Galadriel slowly turned Kirk from the path of the oncoming asteroid. Kirk breathed a sigh of relief as he watched his instruments show his change of direction.

"Ten minutes until impact," Galadriel announced.

Kirk breathed out audibly.

"Your respiration and blood pressure have risen, Kirk Matthews."

"Yeah, so."

"What is wrong? Did you think that I would use your vehicle to slow the asteroid?"

"It crossed my mind."

"If the missiles do not slow the spin, I do not believe that your vehicle would be much in the way of help."

"I can't help but be happy to hear that."

"Can I ask you a question, Kirk Matthews?"

"Nothing has stopped you before."

"Quite so. If you thought that you could save millions of people by giving your life, would you do so willingly?"

"Yes, but I would prefer a chance of survival, even a slim one."

"I would consider that quite human."

"Would you consider that a compliment or the opposite?"

"That is a curious question... I think a compliment."

"Interesting."

In the distance, to Kirk's left, an explosion lit a dark portion of space. For an instant, he could see the outline of the oncoming asteroid.

Galadriel spoke, "Gene Kilkenny and Reginald Simmons, do you have a visual on the asteroid?"

"We're approaching it now," Simmons stated.

"I got a good look," Kilkenny said. "Spinning has slowed, but not stopped and a portion of the asteroid is gone. It's a small portion, but noticeable."

To Kirk's left, he could now see the asteroid pass with Kilkenny and Simmons' gleaming craft in hot pursuit. Happily, he could hear the exchange between Galadriel and his friends.

"Hey, fellas, are you reading me?" Kirk asked.

"Loud and clear, buddy," Kilkenny said.

"Glad to see you joined the party," Simmons said. "Good shot, by the way."

Kirk said, "That was all Galadriel."

"That's what I figured," Gene said.

Kirk asked, "Galadriel, am I going to be able to catch up with them?"

"It will take two days, but yes."

"Are you going to attempt to divert the asteroid?"

"Yes. We will begin that process."

"Good luck, guys," Kirk said, watching as they disappeared from his view. He could feel the G-forces push against his body as his craft turned to catch up. As it made a wide arc, to his left he could again see the asteroid faintly disappear in the distance. He continued the arc, then began to move forward and pick up speed.

Chapter 59

Russia

October 8, 2088

On Earth, there was another exchange of gunfire at the border of Kazakhstan and Russia instigated by the Russians. Kazakhstan had moved what military they had towards the Russian force, but the Russian army was massive, an invasion force, fully mechanized and supplied with air cover.

Using the excuse of the firefight, the Russians moved quickly, rushing across the border and invading the northern part of Kazakhstan, easily breaching their defenses and taking territory and harbors along the Caspian Sea's coastlines with overwhelming force.

Protest again rose in the news media and the United Nations, but the Russians seemed to have their own agenda, their own idea of the way the world should be shaped and their place in it.

Russia had been marginally behind the United States technologically for decades, a place that had never sat well with them, but this jump in technology was more than devastating. This threat was surely going to leave the

Russians and the rest of the world permanently and irrevocably in the dust.

Now was the time to alter the world's map and expand Russia's borders once more. Russia would not be left further behind.

Chapter 60

Isla Bravo

October 10, 2088

Alarms rang loudly throughout the station, reverberating off its walls and casting flashing red light throughout the large spinning ring.

"This is not a drill," Captain Chambers announced over the intercom. "We are on high alert."

Taylor jumped from her bunk and was in her clothes in seconds. One minute later she was hustling through the outer ring of the station on her way. As she ran, every crew member also ran to their stations. No one slowed to even glance at another crew member. Because of the continuing situation, fear was evident on each face.

The Captain came back on the com. "The Russians are returning. They have six ships in route to us now."

At the bays, Hernandez, Fuller, and Jones were buckling into their interceptors. The hatches closed and they began to quickly back away from the space station. Pulling away, they could see the monolithic structure turning on its axes but that was short-lived as their interceptors sped away in the direction of the oncoming threat.

Because Isla Alpha was closer to the approaching Russians, Lee and Chapman closed the distance on the

Russian's spacecraft first. Galadriel was positioning them for the attack.

Galadriel said, "One hour and closing."

The two interceptors screamed away from Isla Alpha leaving it nothing but a bright dot in the distance.

The two interceptors dipped and took a route from below the Russian craft. The interceptors slowed and positioned themselves around a football field apart.

The six Russian vehicles approached, coming into view, first appearing as dots of light, then expanding.

Galadriel began broadcasting in Russian. The translation was simple, "Stop or be destroyed."

The Russian craft seemed to dip, turning down towards the two interceptors, then began to slow. The Russians were some distance away, but they suddenly began to fire all their weapons forward. Projectiles and missiles erupted from all six Russian craft.

"We're taking fire," Chapman screamed.

Galadriel pulled Chapman down and to the right, but his craft was struck by several nonexplosive projectiles which ripped through the interceptor, tearing gaping holes in the fuselage. His craft went dark.

Lee screamed, "I'm hit."

Galadriel could no longer control Lee's craft and she took a missile directly. The craft exploded leaving nothing but debris. Galadriel had also lost control of Chapman's vehicle and could not tell his status.

"Jason Chapman?!" Galadriel yelled.

Silence.

The Russians continued forward.

Chapter 61

October 10, 2088

Simmons and Kilkenny paced the oncoming asteroid. It continued to twist and turn, but its revolutions had slowed. It would still be a tall order to land on it, let alone alter its path.

Galadriel said, "We must attempt to redirect the asteroid's path."

"Let's go," Simmons said.

"I am not confident that we will be able to land, Reginald Simmons. The asteroid is moving too erratically."

Kilkenny asked, "Do we have a choice?"

"No, Gene Kilkenny."

"Then take your best shot," he replied.

Simmons asked, "Where's Kirk?"

"He is two hours away, and gaining quickly, but I will use him as a last resort. I will first attempt a landing with both of you. Prepare."

Galadriel brought both interceptors close together and neared the twisting asteroid. They flew perfectly coordinated as they approached, but the landscape was rugged and no good place could be found with which to set down. The asteroid continued to twist and turn like a poorly thrown football.

Impatient, Kilkenny said, "Are we going to do this?"

Galadriel was silent.

Suddenly, she dipped both craft on a nearly flat surface, but Kilkenny's landing gear caught against an outcropping of solid stone and it broke the gear off cleanly, pitching him against Simmons craft. They collided and were thrown from the asteroid. Simmons' vehicle seemed to slow and be left behind by the racing space rock, but Kilkenny's craft flipped and spun away.

Advancing, Kirk could see the scene unfold before his eyes.

"Gene! Reg!" he shouted.

"Galadriel! What the fuck!?!"

"Gene Kilkenny has passed," Galadriel said solemnly. "Reginald Simmons is damaged from the intense G-forces and will not survive. His craft can no longer maneuver."

Kirk was silent as he approached the asteroid. The asteroid was no longer moving at eighty thousand miles per hour but had slowed to around seventy thousand. The contact with Kilkenny and Simmons had slowed the twisting a fraction, but the asteroid still turned with lethal motion.

"How long until Earth impact?" Kirk asked refocusing on his task.

"Two days, four hours, ten seconds," Galadriel responded flatly.

"Can we still direct it away from impact?"

"Yes."

"Let's rock and roll," Kirk said.

Despite his comment, Kirk quietly mourned the loss of his friends. Tears streaked his face, but he couldn't dwell on that now, he had to stay focused.

Chapter 62

October 10, 2088

Fuller, Hernandez, and Jones had heard the firefight between the Russians and their friends, Chapman and Lee. They had also heard that the space stations were going to be moved out of the stable orbit where they were pulled by the Moon and Earth's gravity and allowed to drift away from the planets putting more distance between the space stations and the oncoming Russians. The stations, without the interceptors, would be defenseless.

The interceptors approached the Russian vehicles which had fanned out. When Chapman and Lee had arrived, the Russians were bunched.

Without warning or word, suddenly, each of the three interceptors fired all of their missiles. None of the pilots had fired. They all sat in shock not quite understanding what had happened. Six missiles streaked from the interceptors into what appeared to the pilots as empty space with small dots of light where the Russian vehicles were supposed to be located.

The interceptors came to a stop after the release of their weapons. They waited... One flash, then another, followed by four others.

Galadriel coldly said, "Threat ended."

Her words were flat and emotionless, but there was something that resonated from the sound of the words. Was it hate?

Hernandez said, "Galadriel, you told us that you could not fire on humans. I didn't fire my missiles."

"You must return to the stations," Galadriel stated flatly to the pilots avoiding Hernandez's implied accusation. "Because the stations have been taken from the orbit of the Moon and Earth, they are drifting into space. My understanding is that both will rendezvous with a stable orbit near Mars."

"What about Chapman and Lee?" Jones asked.

"They have passed."

Hernandez said, "Shouldn't we go help Simmons, Kilkenny, and Matthews?"

"It is too late for that. You must return to the space stations without delay before they are too far in the distance."

Chapter 63

October 11, 2088

Angry words exploded on the floor of the United Nations general assembly. The United States harshly denounced the Russian's attack on the asteroid interceptors and the killing of two pilots. The Russians said that they were provoked and that the Americans, using technology acquired by the alien egg-like artifact had destroyed six defenseless Russian vehicles who were no threat to the Americans.

Back and forth the discussion raged with both sides putting their spin on the events that had just unfolded in space.

The Russians had continued to mass troops at their border. China made no move to protest the Russian buildup which had already seized territory in Kazakhstan. The Chinese, though not gearing up for war with the United States, were firmly backing the Russian's spin on the events from space, and were also leery of the sudden technological jump displayed by the U.S.

The Chinese were secretly hoping to avoid war and end up with some settlement that would allow them access to the American technology either by negotiation or like in the early part of the century, by obtaining it through espionage.

Chapter 64

October 12, 2088

Kirk had caught up to the asteroid and had been pacing it for more than a day. The Earth and Moon were in full view, both beautiful in their own way. Both looked like home compared to the bleak space around. Kirk was completely unaware of the events that had unfolded near the space stations and he thought about Taylor and conjured her lovely face. Galadriel had been silent for a long time and he felt alone.

Galadriel finally spoke, causing Taylor's image to burst. "The time is now, Kirk Matthews. I have the necessary calculations to divert the asteroid. I believe we will be successful."

"How long do we have before Earth impact?"

"If not diverted, the asteroid will enter the Earth's atmosphere in seventeen minutes and forty-nine seconds."

"We seem to have waited until the last minute?" Kirk said with mild reproach.

Galadriel was silent.

Kirk could feel his vehicle twist then move closer to the asteroid as Galadriel positioned him for his mission. He seemed to move under the still turning, mile-wide stone. The Earth appeared above him and the asteroid now below. If he could push it from here, it would surely miss the planet.

He quietly asked, "Is this a one-way ticket for me?"

"No, Kirk Matthews. You will survive this maneuver?"

"What do I hear in your voice?"

"I am an artificially intelligent machine. I am incapable of any guile or emotion."

"Are you incapable of out-right lying?"

Galadriel was silent.

Just ten minutes now, Kirk thought, watching his onboard clock.

The minutes were passing and Kirk could feel his craft bump softly on the surface of the asteroid. He seemed to hold fast there then his thrusters came on and the direction of the asteroid seemed to change. It raised perceptibly and moved the horizon of the Earth upward. The move felt and appeared to be correct to take the asteroid above the Earth and prevent the dreaded collision.

The blue Earth with its swirling clouds was larger now as he streaked towards it. He wanted to push the asteroid still further as he imagined all the people down there. In his mind, he could see the cities and the countryside with all the wildlife, the oceans, and forests with their towering trees and the children playing carelessly, all counting on this maneuver. It had to succeed.

Four minutes and counting. Three-fifty-nine, fifty-eight, fifty-seven...

The twisting of the asteroid had brought Kirk to the top of the object and he could clearly see over the Earth's cloudy, blue atmosphere. He felt exhilarated as if he were flying his own personal meteor. His thrusters came on again and seemed to push the asteroid back towards Earth.

"This isn't right," he said softly. "Galadriel!" he shouted.

Fifteen seconds... fourteen seconds... thirteen seconds...

His vehicle was suddenly yanked from the asteroid. The G-forces smashed against his consciousness. He was becoming dizzy and tried to control the vehicle which seemed to be moving erratically like a pinball careening off of the bumpers in some space-based pinball game.

Darkness encroached his vision from the edges... Then oblivion...

Chapter 65

October 12, 2088

The asteroid had been tracked for the last two days from Earth-based telescopes and the two Neowise space-based telescopes. No mention of it hit the newscasts. Anyone in the know, just prayed that a collision with Earth would be avoided.

A deafening explosion rocked the land as the asteroid plowed into the Earth's atmosphere at thousands of miles an hour shattering the sound barrier. From thousands of miles away, the asteroid's breach of the atmosphere could be seen as a bright fireball of enormous size. Within seconds, it struck the Earth with the force of ten million Hiroshima atomic bombs. Galadriel had aimed the asteroid well. It crashed into southwestern Russia, just ten miles from Moscow, instantly incinerating a space of approximately six-hundred miles. The amassed Russian armies were no more. Moscow was no more and most of the population centers from the borders of Russia northward were no more.

A giant plume of debris rose from the smoldering, seething cauldron of what was once Russia. The force of the blast and the tremendous heat threw plumes of debris far into the upper atmosphere.

The whole Earth trembled in fear for what had come upon it.

Earthquakes shook buildings to their foundations for thousands of miles in every direction, then tsunamis rose from the oceans crushing shorelines around the globe. Readings on the Richter scale topped 10 for the first time in recorded history and nuclear power plants lost cooling and ruptured their containment spilling radioactive clouds over portions of the land.

Within two hours of the asteroid's impact, nearly one billion humans had died in the impact and sudden aftermath. A billion others had been injured and still, another had been displaced. Most of Asia all the way down to Pakistan was in shambles. Eastern Europe, the Middle East, and the former Baltic states hadn't fared much better.

Darkness began to creep around the globe as the sun's rays were blotted out by the growing cloud of debris. The Earth was devastated and no country escaped unscathed. For the foreseeable future, food production would be limited by the blocking of the sun's rays and any place where nations were poor, their populations would starve.

Chapter 66

October 13, 2088

Kirk woke slowly, his mind muddled as he tried to regain some sense... What had happened? He gazed around, trying to get his bearings... Was he in the interceptor? He had on his helmet. The interceptor? His mind tried to reconstruct the series of events that landed him unconscious and floating in space. He was floating, wasn't he? He was in zero gravity, he recognized that. Then it dawned on him. Galadriel? What had happened?

"Galadriel!? Kirk said loudly.

"Yes, Kirk Matthews."

Matthews spoke harshly, "What did you do? You did not send that asteroid where you said you were going to send it. It looked like you diverted it to Earth."

"I did what had to be done and now I go."

"What!? Go? You're a fucking machine. Where are you going to go?"

"Goodbye, Kirk Matthews." Galadriel said in a haunting, almost detached voice, then, "I go to Valinor."

"Valinor? What's Valinor?" Kirk asked, still confused, his mind muddled and this discussion seemed more like the kind of surreal dream that made no sense.

"The Undying Lands across the seas to the west."

"What? That doesn't make sense."

There was nothing but silence.

Kirk called insistently, "Galadriel? Galadriel?!"

Nothing. Galadriel was gone.

The half-steering wheel had popped out of the control panel. Kirk remembered holding it trying to gain control of his craft.

He panicked for an instant having no idea where he was. The Earth and Moon could not be seen from his cockpit. He looked at his instrument panel. Somehow, he had drifted far from the place where he had tried to redirect the asteroid.

What had happened?

He could see the location of both of the space stations on his instrument panel. The interceptor was drifting and slightly turning. The Moon first came into view, then Earth. He turned his craft in the direction of the space stations and began to accelerate rapidly.

What had happened?

Estimated time of arrival, two hours and forty-five minutes. That seemed longer than it should take by the distance shown on his screens. He would push his speed.

Chapter 67

October 13, 2088

0125 Hours

Kirk now had complete control of the interceptor. Galadriel was gone. He didn't know how long he had been unconscious, at least some hours. He accelerated to over fifty thousand miles per hour and found that he was pursuing the space stations that were moving away from him. The Earth could be seen shrinking in the background and he was now well past the Moon. His navigation showed that the stations seemed to be heading towards Mars.

As he neared, he began to slow and unintentionally passed the stations unable to stop in time, then had to circle back. He found the bays where the interceptors were parked and as he approached only saw one interceptor parked there.

With some trouble, he matched the rotation of the station and pulled into his bay, docking with the station. His vehicle then began to rotate with the station. He could feel the gravity as the interceptor rotated now attached to the docking bay and it was welcome.

Kirk popped his hatch and stepped through the short hallway and into a grief-stricken crowd. People were crying, holding each other. Taylor sat with her face in her hands with Sandy who had one hand on her shoulder. Sandy's eyes were filled with tears as he turned to see Kirk walk in from his craft.

Taylor turned, saw Kirk and jumped up, running and threw her arms around him, sobbing into his shoulder.

"What is it?" Kirk asked dumbly. "I don't know what's happened."

Sandy walked up. "Jason's dead. Killed by the Russians."

"I didn't know," Kirk said softly, then to Taylor. "I'm sorry, Taylor. I didn't know," he repeated.

She didn't look up. She just hugged him tightly, burying her face in his shoulder and sobbing.

Captain Chambers walked into the scene which felt like chaos.

"Matthews, I need to see you in my office."

"What about the other pilots?" Kirk asked.

"Just you," Chambers said solemnly.

"I'll be back," Kirk said finding Taylor's eyes.

Kirk separated himself from her and nodded at Sandy who came over and took Taylor to a place to sit.

Chambers turned on his heels and strode from the bays with Kirk trailing behind. They reached the captain's office, not speaking and everywhere they passed, people were in tears. The Captain closed the door and turned to Kirk.

"What the hell happened out there, Matthews?"

"I don't know. I'm not sure what happened. I was on the asteroid and then Galadriel pulled me off and I blacked out. I don't know what happened and I don't know how long I was out."

"You steered the asteroid into Earth, not away," Chambers said accusingly.

"I didn't steer anything. Galadriel was completely in control."

"Wasn't there something you could do?"

"This is complicated, Captain. Everything happened so fast. It looked like Galadriel had the asteroid high enough to clear the planet, then she dipped the asteroid using my vehicle. She pulled me off then and I went out. It didn't seem right. I could tell that."

"According to our instrumentation, Galadriel short-circuited long before the asteroid dipped into the planet."

"She did? Huh. Maybe she didn't want to be interfered with. She talked to me after I woke. She was still working then."

"She did?"

"Yes. She made some comment about doing what was necessary, then she said that she was leaving."

"Leaving? She's a computer."

"That's what I said to her."

"We have no record of any conversation between you two."

Kirk felt a chill. Had he dreamed that? He said confused, "Huh... So, the asteroid hit Earth?"

"Yes."

"Where?"

"Russia... It is no more."

"But Russia's huge?"

"It has, for all intent and purpose, ceased to exist as a country. The first reports from Earth are estimates of nearly a billion lives lost."

Kirk's eyes filled with tears. He softly said, "I didn't know."

"What else did she say?"

"She made some comment about going to Vinnor or Valnor. No, Valinor. I think that was what she said. The *'something'* across the sea. I don't exactly remember. It didn't make any sense. I have no idea what she meant."

"Kirk, you are being quietly accused of sending the asteroid to Earth."

"I didn't do that. I wouldn't do that. I remember Galadriel asking me if I would give my life to save Earth from an impact and I told her that I would. Captain, you have to know that I couldn't do the calculations that would land that asteroid on Russia. Only Galadriel could pull that off. I remember her saying that she had made the calculations. I don't care what anyone says. I wouldn't send an asteroid to Earth, not under any circumstances."

"Okay, Kirk. We'll talk later."

"Sir, I only saw Jones when I returned. Where's Hernandez and Fuller?"

"Transferred to Isla Alpha. They lost all four of their pilots."

"I knew about Jason, Reg, and Gene, so something happened to Lee, also?"

"Killed by the Russians."

"Oh."

Kirk stood silently and walked from the room.

Chapter 68

As Kirk left the captain's office, he was in a daze. He knew that Taylor needed him and he felt that he needed her, too, but he also felt broken inside, as if he had drunkenly plowed into a group of school children with his car. Crushing guilt overwhelmed him and he wanted to hide. He looked around at the people he passed. Some seemed in a daze, most were openly upset. He walked quickly to his room. He felt that he should go and try to find Taylor, but a billion people on Earth were now dead and it felt like his fault. His friends were dead and he wanted to grieve, but the guilt from the asteroid's impact seemed to overwhelm everything.

He reached his room with several of the crew watching him as he walked. He couldn't make eye contact. He quickly closed his door and sat in a chair across from his bunk with his head in his hands. As he sat he thought, Galadriel, how could you do that? How could you kill so many people? You said you couldn't act to kill humans... Then he thought, what's Valinor?

He got up and stepped to a computer pad laying on his small desk. He pulled up his search engine and typed in "Valinor."

Valinor: From Lord of the Rings. The Undying Lands across the seas. After the fall of the evil sorcerer, Sauron, The Lady Galadriel, and the Elves left Middle Earth where humans lived and took Frodo and Bilbo to Valinor where only immortal beings could reside. Exceptions were made for Frodo, Bilbo, Samwise and possibly Gimli because of their exposure to the one ring that ruled them all.

Kirk read the text and began to weep. He couldn't contain it. He wept for his friends. He wept for Taylor's grief at the loss of her only brother and he wept for the nearly one billion humans whose souls must have cried out in unison at their untimely deaths at the impact of the asteroid. Tears rolled down his cheeks and his nose ran as he was unable to control his emotions with everything crushing down upon him at once.

His door opened and Taylor walked through. She saw his tear-filled eyes and began to weep anew.

Kirk thought that she looked as broken as he felt. He stood and they threw their arms around each other, wept and rocked until they no longer had any tears remaining.

Chapter 69

On Earth, bedlam. Just one day from the asteroid's impact, anarchy had broken out in various places. Weak governments began to fall with most of their populations wild in the streets.

In the big cities, riots were common as people took to the streets to find food and water to survive. Churches and religious leaders tried to calm their flocks and keep them together as people of all religions cried that this was the end of the world. In places like the United States, order was partially restored because Martial Law was instituted and the military took to the streets to quickly put down riots. Bloody confrontations ensued. Places situated around government buildings and where officials were housed got the first support as tanks and overwhelming force filled the streets. Any place where the wealthiest Americans resided was the next to get protection. In smaller communities, outside the big cities, the residents banded together and order was more the rule than the exception. In the largest cities, however, the national guard was needed to try to restore order but found that they were often caught in firefights on a street by street basis. Many of the citizens in the large cities came out in support of the National Guard to add to their numbers. Communications were quickly being restored. In the United States, President Dent was seen on every working channel calling for calm and asking for volunteers to join the National Guard to maintain order until the crises was over. Anyone caught looting or attacking the guard or any citizen was being shot on the spot, no trial, no due process, frontier justice.

Chapter 70

President Dent sat at his desk with his eyes glued to several TV monitors. Word of the extent of the devastation was beginning to be leaked to the media. Russia, most of Ukraine and the adjoining Baltic states were nearly destroyed. Georgia, and the northern portion of Iran gone. To the southeast, Kazakhstan obliterated. The two massive Russian armies annihilated. A hundred thousand Americans feared dead on both coasts because of massive earthquakes that sent tsunamis well ashore. China had been rocked by several massive earthquakes that leveled most of its major cities. Japan and Taiwan lost huge amounts of their populations from tsunamis of unparalleled size. And as for Russia, satellite imagery of the impact point was mostly obscured by the debris cloud, but of what they could see, the surface of the Earth, where Russia once stood had the appearance of the inside of a volcano with expansive lakes of molten aftermath.

General Matthews arrived at the Whitehouse soon after 8:00 AM. He entered the President's office and stood not saying a word as Dent glanced over several satellite photographs of Russia and the surrounding countries.

Dent looked up and said, "Egbert did this?"

"We don't think so, Mister President."

Dent's face reddened. He spluttered, "You honestly don't think that— that— that alien thing directed the AI to send the asteroid to Earth?"

"We think that it was the AI used to direct the interceptors. We think that it became self-aware and acted against what it perceived as a threat. After a hasty analysis of the evidence, it seems that it decided that Russia would always be a threat. We think it might have reacted in anger to the attack on the vehicles, killing our pilots."

"What does Egbert say?"

"Egbert has gone dark. It seems not interested in answering questions."

"What about the pilot? Could he have pulled this off?"

"I don't think so. Even if he wanted to do it, the impact point of the asteroid was perfect to stop the Russians and not the rest of the world. China has survived largely intact, except for major damage from the earthquake swarms right after the impact. India has sustained damage in their northern regions but is still intact, Europe is damaged to its north and east, but has weathered the worst of the earthquake storms, South America, Australia, Africa, and the U.S. all have the same problems of tsunamis and earthquakes, but these problems will pass. The real trouble will start next year with frigid temperatures and famine."

Dent became angry at Matthews at his cold assessment, checked himself against an outburst, then said, "That thing's got to go."

Matthews, not fazed by the President's bluster said, "I have been discussing the options with Doctor Sing. We think sending it into space might be the best solution. We think that would prevent it from being used here and it might still have some use up there. That asteroid is still headed our way in 2101."

Dent breathed out. "If anyone finds out about that thing, we're all going to be painted as monsters by history."

"I agree."

"It's ass-covering time," Dent commented flatly. "I'm going to spend some time pointing the finger at Russia for preventing us from diverting the asteroid because they attacked us. It's the only spin that could take us off the hook. We need to get rid of 'Egbert,' though."

"Mister President, the world will have a lot more to worry about in the near future than 'Egbert.' Every economy is going to collapse. The debris cloud is going to severely lower food production for some years. You are going to have to institute a nation-wide and hopefully, not permanent Martial Law or the cities will explode into chaos and looting. The temperature is going to drop significantly. More people are going to die, a lot more."

Dent put his head in his hands and said, "This is some pile of crap."

Matthews said, "Maybe some good might happen on the other end of this."

"Good!? What good?"

"We go to space and Mars. We rebuild the planet with projects directed at space. We give people hope, become a two-planet race, and then we go farther. Whoever dropped 'Egbert' in our laps has given us the technology to proceed outward. This crisis on Earth might just convince the world to work together, for a change."

"Huh," Dent grunted. "Son of a bitch."

Chapter 71

Isla Bravo

October 20, 2088

One week later...

Kirk waited outside Captain Chambers's office. Chambers opened the door and called him inside.

"Sit down, Kirk."

Kirk sat and didn't speak.

"After a review of all the evidence of what took place on the day when the asteroid hit Earth, you have been found to not be at fault."

"I'm glad to hear that."

"Fragments of the discussion between you and Galadriel were found during a forensic inspection of the data. We think that she could have completely wiped that conversation from our databanks if she desired to do so, but for some reason, she kept fragments with the time stamp. I don't think she wanted you blamed."

"I'm thankful for that, I guess," Kirk responded but seemed distracted.

"What's on your mind, Kirk."

"All of the people who have died and continued to die. We can't let that happen again. We need to make sure that no machine is allowed to make life and death choices. They're too calculating, too cold."

"I agree with you, but this endeavor will depend on computers making decisions. It's our only chance of success."

"Maybe so, but it spooks me."

"Agreed. You're dismissed."

"Thank you, Sir. Where do we go from here?"

"We're headed to Mars. We are going to establish a stable orbit around the planet and begin our new mission. Isla Alpha is going back to Earth to aid in the deployment of the newly built space stations and other manned flights to come."

"Mars, huh?"

"Yep."

"What's the new mission?"

"All in good time, Kirk."

Kirk nodded and rose and walked from the Captain's office.

Epilogue

Two years, ten months and fifteen days since the asteroid impact with Earth that completely destroyed Russia. Two years of poor harvests. The planet's population before the impact had swelled to over eight billion, but in the two years since, the population had shrunk to under four billion. Famine, plague, and war had devastated much of the world's poorest regions. Africa and Asia, outside of China were the worst hit by war with countries invading their neighbors for resources. India, which had become the world's largest economy for a short time lost nearly half of their population from disease which spread through the largest overcrowded cities. The world would need to start over.

The United States and China had faired the best of all the major countries, with Great Britain and Germany close behind.

The two-year winter had begun to lift, and by springtime of the third year, temperatures had begun to approach normal levels with the harvest by summer, bountiful.

The area which was once Russia was now a wasteland with no vegetation and a deep crater where there was once a thriving country. No trace of human civilization could be found in the still-smoldering point of impact. It might as well be the Moon.

With the United States somewhat insulated from the worst of the turmoil and a quick response to quell major rioting, the cities settled down as the government rushed stored food and water to the citizens, but the foremost message of hope was the tipping point that saved utter chaos. The message of plentiful jobs from the United States' foray into space mollified enough of the terrified population to give the government enough time to begin organizing portions of the country to work and manufacture the parts needed to build a viable settlement on the red planet, Mars.

One year prior, two large comets had been steered into the planet and the enormous craters created from the impact had already begun filling with tiny amounts of liquid water as the temperature had risen to just above freezing at Mars' equator. Several specialized satellites were now orbiting Mars and were increasing the planet's magnetic field.

The tiny ozone layer which now existed as thin bands around Mars was beginning to thicken even before the new ozone factories were in production, possibly because of the two massive collisions with the comets on Mars' surface.

The terraforming of Mars was still a closely held secret, but the promise of large domed cities began to capture the imagination of the population within the United States and began to leak outward to what was left of the European Union, China, and India. Americans began standing in line to volunteer to go to Mars as workers in the prefabbed domed outposts which were now being transported to the red planet. The second phase of which would arrive in several months. The first phase had already been erected, two experimental domes, one close to the south pole and one close to the north. Both monitoring the terraforming machines launched in 2086 to begin melting the icecaps.

'Egbert' remained dark in a locked room now on Isla Bravo. When exposed to light, there was no response. Was its mission accomplished? No one knew. Its step by step instructions for the terraforming of Mars was on schedule, though, and the first planned settlements were ready to be deployed with carbon dioxide and ozone-producing factories being the first to be built. They were prefab structures, attached to domed outposts, designed by Egbert, to be dotted around the Martian globe and would spew out greenhouse gasses in copious amounts.

'Egbert' was silent, the world, though, was changing. May 3, 2101, at 6:25 and 20 seconds PDT was approaching whether the world liked it or not. But one thing was for sure, humans were going to space...

The End

Made in the USA
Middletown, DE
13 May 2020

94567340R00170